DEAD KACHINA MAN

DEAD KACHINA MAN

by
Teresa VanEtten

Sunstone Press
Santa Fe, New Mexico

All of the characters, places, and incidents in this book are fictitious. Any resemblance to anyone living or dead is purely coincidental. This novel is a figment of the author's imagination only.

Many thanks to Marcia Muth, James Smith, Joseph Szimhart, T. Roy Chan, Michel and Barbara Pijoin, Ed and Lamoine VanEtten, Maynard and Carolyn Herem, Black Bart, and my best friend Thomas E. VanEtten.

First Edition

Printed in the United States of America

Library of Congress Cataloging in Publication Data:

VanEtten. Teresa. 1951—
    Dead kachina man.

    1. Title.
PS3572.A4365D4   1986   813'.54   85-17162
ISBN: 0-86534-072-2

Published in 1986 by SUNSTONE PRESS
                Post Office Box 2321
                Santa Fe. NM 87504-2321/USA

Friday, Day 1

Dominique Rios smiled. Marge turned fifty last night and they told the children not to come. Marge was beautiful, unchanged since they married thirty-two years ago. They celebrated with a quiet dinner, just the two of them in a prolonged evening romance.

His steps echoed down the hall. The phone was ringing. Maybe it was something important. The last three weeks had been quiet, too quiet. He hurried into his office, picked up the phone.

"Jerez Police Department, Captain Dominique Rios speaking."

It was Ed Cruz from San Jaime Pueblo. They had a body, cause of death questionable. Cruz asked if Rios could come up right away.

Captain Rios put the receiver down and walked over to his grey filing cabinet. He opened the top drawer, pushed the dirty brown files back. He hadn't had to use Doc as a medical examiner in so long he wasn't sure of the number. Rios pulled a chart, a number was printed on top.

The ZIA Police had not called for outside assistance in some time. They preferred to work on their own secrets. To the outsider, the Pueblo was a peaceable kingdom. There were no outward signs of violence, the people civilized and cultured. The only problem was an occasional drunk. The ZIA knew how to handle their silent disasters, their quiet rapes. Rios remembered the naked blonde woman found floating downstream. Rios was only twenty then, in his first year out. The bleached blonde, puffy, bruised, unidentifiable had floated out of his grip onto the dry river bed of the Pueblo. The murder was handled by the cigar smoking, thick, black haired ZIA Captain. Cigar drool mingled with his judgement of accidental death. Another pretty blonde was soon seen riding in the mayor's limo.

Rios waited for Doc Tapia to finish his rounds at the dull grey hospital. Both men were quiet as they drove down the flat road to the Pueblo that lay thirty miles from Jerez.

The plains were flat between the mountain ranges that separated this country from the rest of the world. The mountains were high and had snow on them year round. Scrawny pinon trees dotted the plains. Rios and Doc were the only ones on the road and the only other life forms in sight were the cows looking for food in the pinons.

"Who died?" Doc asked, tucking his tie into his pin striped vest. He felt out of place in Captain Rios' battered Chevy pickup truck.

"Someone called Ray Hava. I never knew him, but he was big in the *Indian Forerunner Newspaper* as the best kachina doll carver in the country. Cruz seems to think there's foul play. A lot of Indians competed against Hava."

Captain Rios reached into his cowboy shirt pocket for a cigarette, then he remembered how Doc gave lectures about not smoking. He scratched his neck instead and gave a sigh of relief. The wind picked up, blowing the truck around.

At last things were happening. This challenge excited Rios and action was what he lived for. He always felt guilty when he found the murderer, almost as if it was his fault. His wife never pressed him about his cases and somehow she understood his moods of depression when a case was solved.

Cruz was standing in front of the Mercantile in the center of the Pueblo when they drove up. His old straw cowboy hat was stained with sweat, his jacket flapped in the wind. Cruz always had a cigarette hanging out of his mouth, as if it were part of his body. He was in charge of policing the land just outside the Pueblo for the Jerez Police Department, reporting to Captain Rios.

Cruz was tall for an Indian, over six feet. His face was browned leather, dark chocolate eyes peered out from creases around cheeks and nose. He was thin, rugged, and crude, too crude at times, a walking flag pole, with a bad mouth.

The Pueblo was guarded by it's own police force, the ZIA Police. They made it clear that they did not want the Jerez Police on their land or in their business. Rios was unsure of his involvement in this case. If Cruz was in the Pueblo waiting for him, then the call for help was legitimate.

"Doc, Captain Rios, something is wrong. I'm not sure what, but things don't make any sense. This guy was fine yesterday. He works here at the Mercantile and everyone in the Pueblo saw him. He just died sometime last night. He had a physical just three months ago. He went to Mexico City for the Indio show. Come, take a look."

Rios had rarely seen an Indian upset. Usually they were so calm and unruffled that it would drive anyone else crazy. But Cruz was walking fast and seemed to feel a real sense of urgency. Rios looked around him. The wind tossed whirlwinds of dirt at the brown mud houses. Doors and window frames were painted wth turquoise blue paint, each a different shade.

The short houses had straw worked into the adobe mud walls. The sun reflecting on this golden straw gave the houses the appearance of being gold filled. Some had strings of chilis hanging from round vega endings that stuck out from the roof. Others had braided colored corn.

Two houses on the end were beautifully shaped, built during the Spanish conquest. Oval windows with carefully fitted iron bars had been a curiosity to many visitors to the Pueblo. Skinny dogs lay against the sun warmed walls.

People were going in and out of the house as they approached. The women coming out were solemn, their wraps pulled up around brown faces with brown bangs. Children were smoking outside the house and there were cars parked right at the door. Perhaps the dead man could talk.

Cruz had not followed police procedure. Rios frowned. Doc grumbled under his breath.

As Cruz arrived at the blue door everyone stepped back. He yelled at someone. A tall Indian came out, red bandana around his head, blood coming out of his nose. There had been a fight in the house. Cruz picked up a short man and threw him into the dusty road. Doc was quiet.

Doc was half-Spanish and half-Anglo and the people around him were a challenge. They drank too much, smoked too much, and in general were unhealthy by their own hand. He didn't mind taking care of these people as long as he didn't have to live with them. Doc loved medicine and he had reached a few of the Indians. The majority were stuck in their ways.

A woman with short black bangs and a red shawl came out of the house, her eyes were amber and she was pale, a gentle smile on her face. She walked over to Doc and studied him cautiously. Doc put his hand out. She grasped it for a moment and then let it drop.

"I am Evelyn Hava." Her manner was shy, her stature small, her face beautiful. She was in her late thirties or early forties. Her feet were bundled in moccasins, her dress a soft purple paisley print. Self-assurance complimented the quizzical shyness.

"Would you like to come in? The house is full of people, please excuse the clutter."

Mrs. Hava moved in little steps, oriental style, stooped when she spoke in a whisper voice. Rios smiled.

"Please excuse my sons, they are mad. They want to kill someone. Ray had just come home three nights ago. He had come home with a lot of money. My sons are convinced that some old drunks killed him trying to get it."

She stood aside and let the men enter the house. Her soft hand brought up a pointed finger showing the direction of the bedroom and the dead body. Tears welled in the corners of her sharp eyes.

Rios removed his brown Stetson hat. Thick greying brown hair framed his tanned face, grey-blue eyes scanned the room. He walked ahead of Doc. "Do you think Cruz has been through here already?" He thought, Indians stuck together no matter what their differences. Rios felt like a common enemy their alliance would resist.

He went up to the body. Doc followed closely behind him, "I'm sure Cruz has taken a look."

The body was in bed, covers up to the chin. The man appeared asleep, hair dark black and mussed. Doc opened his black bag quietly.

Rios glanced at the bedside table made of warped plywood on three cinder blocks, painted brown. There was a picture of Mary and Jesus, a chipped glass of water, some black sewing thread, an account book in a covered plastic envelope. Rios pushed the account book into a plastic bag and placed the remaining items into a larger plastic pouch he pulled from his jacket pocket.

"Smell something unusual in here?" Rios looked at Doc, a foreigner on foreign land performing a duty.

Doc sniffed and nodded 'yes'.

Doc lifted up the dead man, bending him over a thin cot that served as a bed. Rios watched. Doc slapped the man hard on the back. Taking a large wad of white fluffy cotton, he pushed it inside the man's mouth, pulled it out, and dropped it into a brown bottle. He lay the man down again with a thud, the cot tilted lifting dust from the mud floor. A fly buzzed.

Cruz walked in, cigarette smoke spewing out of his mouth, "Did you find anything?" He snorted and spat into the corner of the room.

Rios shook his head, "No chance yet to inspect his belongings. This room is neat compared to the other one," his chin jerked in the direction of the thick pine door.

Cruz leaned against the dry mud wall. His dirty dark leather vest hung loosely over a torn faded brown jacket. He stuck his yellow calloused hand into a worn blue jean pocket, scuffed dirty brown boots pointed at Rios.

"Well, the ZIA and me have gone through every damn thing we felt was related to the murder."

Rios turned his back on him, "And what did you find that was related to the murder?"

Cruz coughed. Doc stood up and gave Rios a warning frown. Cruz pulled the cigarette from his tobacco stained lips, "Whatever we found, I turned over to the ZIA."

Rios lifted his eyebrow, "The ZIA?" he said with disgust as he lifted a photo from the bureau. "Cruz, you told me they called us in to investigate. If that's true, then any evidence should stay with us. They felt this murder had outside influences and we can't solve anything if we don't have clues. Now can we?" Rios noticed the picture was Ray Hava standing in front of the Indio flag.

Hava had been a tall man with thick black hair cut very short. One eye was looking at the camera and the other was almost shut from squinting. He was holding a large kachina doll with a blue ribbon. His nose was bent, perhaps broken several times, hands small and delicate. Hava's suit shined, his collar buttons flapped over. He must not have been used to wearing suits. There were obviously two people standing on either side of him but he couldn't see them since the picture was cut to fit the frame. Rios put the picture down and walked to the window.

"Do you remember what you found with the ZIA men?"

Cruz shifted his weight and stared in Rios' eyes. He stuck the cigarette back in his mouth and grunted, "No."

Rios turned back to the window, and stood with his feet apart, hands resting solidly in his back pockets. His long thin body blocked the yellow light from the deep set wooden window. He stole a glance at Cruz. The smell in the room was oily, like incense or burned meat. The window was shut tight, yellow plastic on the outside to seal it. He felt along the ledges on the inside. No one could come in or out of this window, he was sure. Below, a wooden chest was covered with a frayed Indian blanket. At the side lay ceremonial leggings. A kilt embroidered with bright red and green colors with thin quills hung from the side of a bureau.

All around the leggings were dried pinon needles that had fallen from a branch that lay across a beam under the window. Rios again noticed the photo on top of the bureau.

The two people on either side of Hava in the photo were probably women. There was a pink skirt showing by his leg and Hava's arm holding the kachina doll had a woman's hand on its sleeve. It wore a wedding ring. Mrs. Hava would have certainly seen the photo.

Doc finished his examination of the body and took the cup of water by the bed and lifted it up with his fingers inside the cup. He poured the water into a bottle. Then he pulled out a plastic bag and dropped the cup into it. He held it out for Rios. Rios took the bag and glanced at the body. In the light he could now see that Ray Hava had a pained expression on his face — something he had not noticed before.

The corpse had not started to smell, yet something certainly did smell.

"Doc, what is that stink?"

Doc shook his head. Rios walked out of the room brushing Cruz as he passed. The front room was crowded, people were crying, women cooking in the kitchen, men in quiet conversation, shaking their heads and speaking of Evelyn. Ray Hava was no longer their concern.

Rios moved from person to person. The conversations were concerned for Evelyn and her future. Rios examined the room: pictures on the walls were religious in cheap plastic frames, but one photo of Hava in front of the Mercantile with some other people showed Evelyn in her wedding dress. Hava and Evelyn stood apart, separated.

There were kachina dolls on the fireplace hearth. They were not placed evenly, or maybe one was missing. On the banco were leggings, a shovel by the front door, and a matate and mano next to a rocking chair.

The smell in the bedroom was not noticeable in the front room.

Doc pushed his way through the crowd, "Rios, ready to go? I got all I can right now." He mumbled under his breath as he neared Rios, "If Evelyn signs for an autopsy, we can do that at the hospital."

Outside, the ZIA Policemen were showing some children new two-way radios in the shiny brown ZIA cars. Doc shook his head and walked around them. He looked like a very old man, bent and withered from another time and another place, caught in a deep frown. Rios pulled the truck door open for him.

"Cheer up Doc, it's not you lying dead." Doc kept his frown and climbed into the truck. The ride back was slow.

"Did you notice Ray Hava's kachina dolls?" Doc asked.

Rios pulled the sunvisor down, "Yes, I saw three on the hearth in the front room."

Doc put his elbow on his black bag, "I have one of his, come to think of it. My wife fell in love with one she saw at the Mercantile. Hava had a way of making their expressions so life-like. The bodies on the dolls are basic, not too dramatic, but the faces speak out. Don't you think?"

"They do have a human appearance. How expensive are they?" Rios hadn't really given them much thought.

Doc shrugged, "We got ours in trade. Thinking of buying one?"

Rios turned in the seat, shifting his weight, "No. Just wondered if there was market for them. This is a pottery Pueblo isn't it?"

Doc answered, "Rios, nowadays anything that is authentically Indian costs a lot of money. Indians are now getting paid handsomely for their arts. I have no idea what a kachina doll costs. But if Hava was as famous as the *Indian Forerunner* said, his dolls are worth a lot."

Rios down shifted, "Is there any reason why he would give a kachina to the ZIA?"

Doc sighed, "Who knows? Maybe his wife did."

Rios rolled down the window. "Maybe."

The weather was agreeable now but the mountains were lost in dark clouds.

"What was that smell in the bedroom?" Rios pulled out a cigarette and lit up, suddenly uncomfortable. He'd never trusted doctors, as a patient or an equal.

Doc breathed a sigh, "I think it was some kind of incense. I've smelled something like it before. I'm trying to remember where." Doc scratched the back of his hand. "That man had only been dead about six hours. Must have died early this morning."

Rios pushed his hat back. It was then he noticed a large burn across the back of Doc's hand. He was sure it wasn't there on the way out. Sudden nervousness overcame Doc's usual calm intellectual coolness. He was perched on the edge of the truck seat, vulnerablility beginning to show.

Rios unbuttoned his levi jacket. "It's strange to think of all those people in that house. Anyone of them could have taken anything at anytime and no one would have noticed. Do you think his wife would have noticed her husband choking to death next to her?"

Doc rolled down his window, "She's a strange one. She didn't let on she knew what happened at all."

Rios inhaled. "What do you know about Indian Death. Dead is dead. Do you think Hava was murdered?"

Doc's deepset brown eyes sparkled, "Yes, I do." Rios pulled up to the dull grey Hospital Emergency Room entrance.

"Call me if you find something, or even if, well, you don't...call me." Doc hurled himself against the truck door. It creaked open and Doc and his black bag smelling of alcohol solution disappeared through the double doors, escaping.

Rios turned and drove down the long driveway from the hospital. The sun shone through the poplar trees, small black clouds drifted across the blue sky. Hava's face came to mind. It strained against something, hands clenched and held fast to the side of the cot. There were no wounds. A flock of crows flew high over the truck. Certainly Hava must have jumped or called out. If he couldn't breathe, he must have grabbed the sheets as he passed on to the next life. Lightning flashed across the mountains as Rios drove up to Police Head-quarters.

Later he sat at his worn pine desk heaped with stacks of files and mixed reports and held the report in his long brown fingers. Cause of death: unknown. The water had checked out okay, so it wasn't poison. And he had not been strangled although there seemed to be something wrong with the tissues of his throat. Doc said the only apparent way of death was suffocation. A man suf-focated all by himself. Strange.

Rios walked out into the musty hall. "Carl, get in here. I need your university psychology."

Carl was about six feet tall with a high forehead and thick glasses. He was dressed in a red corduroy long sleeved shirt with creased blue jeans covering his black boots.

"I brought you some coffee. Here's the report Doc sent Cruz. Oh, I see you already got it. Well..."

Rios took the mug with some hesitancy, and pushed a chair over to him. "How does a man die from suffocation if no one strangled him and he didn't choke?"

Rios put the coffee to his lips. Coffee was a strong point in Rios' life. Good coffee was like a good cigar, it was something you guarded well.

Carl sat down, "It would have to be either from choking or maybe some kind of epileptic fit."

Choking was what Rios had thought, but Doc said it wasn't plausible. The man's esophagus was clear, and his stomach was empty so there was nothing to cause choking or gagging. And if he had choked it would have awakened his wife. Smoke was also ruled out because no one else had any symptoms.

"There is no evidence that anything was stuck in his windpipe to cause him to gag and then choke." Rios walked around his desk and sat down. A car below backfired setting off a chorus of barking dogs and loud remarks.

"As for epilepsy, we have two doctors who examined him just this year and he never had any signs. Hava was in the Navy for five years and he was never diagnosed as an epileptic. The Navy is very careful about that kind of thing. So what do you think?" Rios leaned back putting his feet on the desk.

Carl shook his head, "The only other thing I can figure is something I learned since I got out of school. It's far-fetched and psychologically possible, but highly improbable."

"All right, go on."

"Well, you may laugh at this. It's only lately that doctors are beginning to accept this in the South Sea Islands and they still question it. But there's evidence that a religious belief can kill."

Carl stood up, walked to the door and pushed it shut. The tin knob jerked out then fell into position with a soft click.

Rios was not ready for a lecture on the deaths of religious Indians in the South Sea Islands. They were too far away to imagine.

Rios smiled and nodded to the chair, "Carl, get on with it?"

"There is a study that people can be killed by a belief if they have believed in it all their life and accept it as a form of punishment or righteousness."

Rios put his coffee mug down, "This is a police matter. If and when we find the murderer, Carl, we will have to take our evidence to court. What you're talking about doesn't sound like it would hold up as concrete evidence. If you're talking about a hypothetical situation in some other land, then I think you're wasting your time and mine."

Carl stood up, "Yes, Sir. You're right, it probably wouldn't pertain to this case at all."

He put his chair in the corner and moved for the door.

Rios put his hands up, "What did you find out on the items I brought you from Hava's house?"

Carl shrugged, "Well, the fingerprints were Hava's on the account book and the picture of Mary and Jesus was smeared with a number of prints. The account book was in a plastic container, as you know. There were no definite marks on it. He didn't have much money. All in all nothing. Nothing as far as evidence, concrete evidence, that is." Carl pulled open the door and walked down the hall.

The Court was in Alcala two hours away, with paved streets, first-class hotels, and signal lights. It also had a first-rate police force.

Rios stopped at the Mexican Cafe on the corner and called Marge from the pay phone to tell her about the case.

Rios hung up and walked to a table. Four waitresses stuffed into stained light blue uniforms came up to him at once. "There is news that a killer is on the loose, is it true?" Rios let his eyes adjust to the dimly lit room. The curtains were pulled, pinned, dirty red squares blocked the sunlight.

Rios took his hat off, "Don't know of a killer, do you?"

The bright ruby red lips frowned, blue, green, and brown eyeshadow appeared on disappointed eyes. It would make juicy gossip if Rios let them in on it.

Rios smiled, clapping his hands together, "Where's my bowl of chili?" The waitresses flitted away to the kitchen, replaced by a large red headed woman. The floor shook as she sat down abruptly on the wooden chair. "Rios, we hear there was a death at San Jaime Pueblo. It was good old Ray Hava. Do you think he was murdered?" The fat woman put her sweaty head into her hand which leaned on a wrinkled red arm braced against the table.

"Red, it's mysterious what goes on in the world." Rios lit up a cigarette, watching her over the match smoke.

"Rios, Hava was a good man. He come in here a lot with his wife, sometimes with other women. If he would have only glanced in my lonely direction. Hava was a Hano that married hardhearted women. Yes, Hava liked to feel good. Poor man deserved it. He made himself happy, not too many tried to make him feel good for good feelings sake, you know?" Tears trickled down her cheeks.

"Hava was a quiet man until you got him going. Then he would laugh and everyone around him would laugh. He wanted to be happy, that's all he wanted. He had a rough life." Red wiped her eyes. "It's too hot in here for me. What do you think about the color of this room?" She glanced at the walls.

Rios studied the walls. "What do you want me to say?"

"You should be honest with me, what do you think about the color?"

Rios took the cigarette from his lips, "Stained."

Red smiled, "I thought so, Rios, you good-looking cop. Too bad you're married. You know fat people get lonely?"

Rios put his hand on the wrinkled arm, "I know somewhere in there is a beautiful thin woman that would shock the world. Were you ever lonely enough to find out more about Hava?"

Red blushed and turned to a waitress. "Rosa, where is the Captain's chili, the man is hungry, pronto."

Rios finished his lunch and walked out into the sunshine. He put on his dark glasses that reflected the brown town around him. Rios had just enough time to get the truck's timing fixed and get out to San Jaime before four o'clock and home in time for a late dinner with Marge.

Dirt blew against the truck. A group of farmers trudged by, each waving a worn brown hand, their hats banded with sweatstains, their blue jeans worn to a perfect fit. Their faces brown and wrinkled, snarls of determination in set expressions. The apple crops must be in, that was the only time the farmers came to town. Their women stayed home immersed in apple pies, applesauce, apple butter, and children with stomach aches.

* * * * * *

9

Rios drove through the Pueblo. It was quiet enough for six o'clock. There were a few drunks leaning against the post office. Rios pulled up in front of the Mercantile, a tall building two stories high and as long as two city blocks. The San Jaime Mercantile sign was newly painted.

Rios remembered when he had tried to paint the trim that ran along the top of his own house and kept falling off the ladder. He was luckier than most for he had caught hold of the fire wall all three times and had never actually fallen. Whoever painted the sign on the Mercantile must have been a professional or had no fear of heights and death.

He let the truck roll up along the cement walk next to the store. He parked it in gear, the emergency brake needed fixing, and went up the steps. Ray Hava had come up these very steps to work everyday for three years, full of life. The inside was all lit. The last time Rios was here was about six years ago. It was then dark and dirty. Now it was clean, smelled good, respectable. There were several Indians standing in line buying food, a butcher was cutting meat in the back.

Rios took his dark glasses off, tucking them in his work shirt pocket. "Hey, we close in five minutes," a lady behind the display cases yelled to him. She pushed her long black hair back behind her ears to reveal silver squash blossom earrings. He walked over, showed her his Jerez Police Badge and I.D. and asked for the owner.

The lady straightened and hesitated, "Is this about Ray Hava?"

"Yes."

"Is there a problem?" she asked, putting her hands on her silver concho belt.

Rios smiled a faint smile, repeated himself firmly, "Who owns this store and can I speak to him?" She didn't move, set grin covered with blood red lipstick.

He walked over to an old wooden railed post office grill and leaned over. There was a man behind the grill at a desk.

"Excuse me, I am Captain Rios of the Jerez Police Department. I've been asked by the ZIA to investigate a case. I need to speak to the owner of the store."

The man stood up, put out his hand. "I am Mr. Quintana and I own and run this store. Please, how can I help you?"

Rios asked about Ray Hava and how long Mr. Quintana had known him. Were there any personal problems that Ray Hava had lately and did he have any enemies.

Mr. Quintana answered carefully, almost deductively, almost memorized.

"Is there a problem about answering these questions?" Rios put it to him straight.

Mr. Quintana nervously glanced around. His photogrey glasses slid down his nose. "Cruz was in here this morning and he asked all of us these questions that you have asked. He told us to tell you just certain things when you came in to question us, or else…''

Rios stood back, studying the man from head to foot. Mr. Quintana was about forty-five, hair cut short, his clothes were Ivy League, brown penny loafers barely stuck out from under brown corduroy pants. He looked like a college professor, certainly not the kind of man who was easily intimidated.

In theory, Cruz worked for Rios and was supposed to confirm all investigations with him. What was going on? Cruz had been rattled this morning when they came to see the body, but this was uncalled for. Cruz had no authority in the Pueblo, only in Jerez.

''Mr. Quintana, is there a place where I can talk to you alone?''

Mr. Quintana stood and walked through the swinging door of the wooden post office grill. ''Lilly, I will be in the back if you need me. You and Charles close up the front.''

Mr. Quintana pointed to a young Spanish boy wearing a long dark blue denim apron. ''Charles, you better close the door, it's getting late.'' Mr. Quintana nodded his head towards the back and Rios followed. Maybe, now they could get somewhere. They walked past the meat department, around a kitchen, through a thick adobe doorway to the back bowels of the store.

It was dimly lit and two silversmiths were working on jewelry, a potter was throwing pots on a spinning board. Rios was amazed at all the rooms in the store. It was like a cave. The windows were high, up next to the ceiling, walls rough mud three feet thick or more, old wooden plank floors scrubbed clean. They shone in the light from the high windows. Light bulbs hung all the way down to their level from the ceiling.

''Through here, to the kaleidoscope factory. They close at five, so there's no one here now. Just let me look around and see if they've all gone and the intercom is off.''

The factory was full of cardboard that soared up into vigas at the top of the store, rolls of colored paper were stacked all about. Glass triangles lay on tables and mirrors hung along the inner wall. There was an office in the back. The transformation from Trading Post to modern kaleidoscopes was startling.

Rios sat down in one of the worker's secretarial padded chairs to wait. On a work table was a photo of a woman standing in front of the Indio flag. It looked just like the photo he had seen in the Hava house. And it too had been cut to fit the frame: a black metal five by seven frame.

''There, now we can talk.'' Mr. Quintana sat down in a chair next to the table that had the photo.

''Do Indians work here in the factory?''

''Yes, they have worked here for as long as the factory has been here. They were here when we took over the store.''

Rios had never heard of Indians making kaleidoscopes. Quintana told him that not too may outsiders knew what went on inside this Pueblo. It was very closed socially and politically. The kaleidoscopes were made here and then shipped out all over the world. They put an address on the outside of them which was a business mailing address in Florida. So there was no way of tracing the kaleidoscopes to the Pueblo.

Rios asked him if the owners were legitimate and Quintana seemed to feel they were or he wouldn't have allowed them to continue in the store. They had all their workers insured and made sure they were treated fairly. They paid the legal minimum wage and even gave Christmas bonuses.

Mr. Quintana had owned the store for four years now and had come into the Pueblo with the best of intentions. He and his wife had lived on other reservations, they both had been teachers. Mr. Quintana hesitated over the last sentence, his ears turning red.

When his wife turned thirty, he explained, she inherited a large sum of money. They bought this store because the two of them loved the change of work and the people. They had cleaned up the store and given the local people jobs. They even helped the Indians rekindle their love for pottery making and helped the women sell their wares in Jerez and San Joaquin. They had also loved Ray. Ray was not from this Pueblo. Quintana hesitated. Quintana was lying, his eyes jumping around the room.

Rios pulled out his notes. "Ray Hava was a Hano Indian, wasn't he? Don't the women in the Pueblos bring their husbands back to live in their Pueblos. Somewhere I understood that if a woman marries a man from another Pueblo, he is obligated to go and live in his wife's Pueblo with her family."

Mr. Quintana smiled. "Yes, the Pueblos are female oriented."

Rios flipped some pages in his note pad, "What does a woman do if she finds out her husband is fooling around on her?"

Mr. Quintana frowned, "That doesn't happen too often." He sat up straight, crossing his legs.

Rios frowned, "What then, the wives fool around on their husbands?"

Mr. Quintana responded, "More than likely." He cleared his throat.

Rios stretched his long legs out in front of him. "If a man were to do something of what I said, what would happen?"

Quintana held his breath. Rios pressed him, "Do they have some kind of policing system that works socially, like the Mud Men?"

Quintana leaned back in his chair, fingers tracing the outline of the work table, "Yes they do. It is not something to push. It is very strict and secretive. I wouldn't want to get on their bad side." Sweat beaded on his forehead.

Rios nodded, "You mean like the Klu Klux Klan?"

Mr. Quintana looked down, "Well, maybe not that radical, but, yes, something like it."

Rios wrote in his note pad. "Would they have killed Ray Hava if they knew that he was fooling around on his wife? She is a favorite in the Pueblo?"

Quintana picked up a pencil, "Well, I wouldn't want to say. They are a serious organization. I have never heard of them killing, that is a steep step to take, even for them."

Rios pushed his hair back from his forehead, it was time for a haircut. "Tell me about Hava?" His voice loud and squeaky.

Quintana explained, "Ray had grown up in Hano. Just as you said. He had come from a proud family that held a lot of elders in leading tribes. Ray's mother was Zuni. Unlike the Pueblo Indians, she went to live with her husband's people. She wanted Ray to leave the Hano land, there was always fighting between the tribes."

Quintana brushed some lint off his pant leg. "She had saved a lot of money from her blanket weavings and had sent him off to Gallup when he was fifteen to help his uncle who worked at a trading post. That is where he learned to carve and became an expert in the art of making kachina dolls. He had taken his work to the Gallup ceremonials and met a beautful young girl named Sofie."

Quintana stopped. Perhaps he had gone too far.

"Sofie was the mother of four children when she married Ray. Is that correct?" Rios pointed his pencil at Quintana.

"She was definitely a package deal. He was married to her for more than six years." Quintana wiped his brow.

Rios pulled out a cigarette, "Was she from here?" He lit it.

Quintana frowned, "Don't you have that in your notes?" Rios smiled.

"I would like to be sure." Rios blew out the match, searching for a place to discard it. Quintana lifted his eyebrow, "Yes, she was from here. She had several more children after she married Hava. Although none of them looked to be his. They were all different and one was black as night. The middle daughter was beautiful and Ray was fond of her. He would buy her special things from the store and even got Doc to check her over and give her birth control so she wouldn't end up like her mother." Mr. Quintana glanced at his watch.

Rios coughed and cleared his throat, "What happened to her?"

"She joined the Air Force and last I heard she was in flight training school in Germany."

Rios put his note pad in his pocket, "How did Hava meet Evelyn?"

Quintana smiled, "Ray got a job here at the store and worked for about three years. He wanted a divorce since Sofie had finally run off with a candy machine man and was living with him in Alcala. The kids were all grown and old enough to look after themselves." Quintana sighed, tired of the interrogation.

He took off his glasses, rubbed his eyes, turquoise inlay bolo tie fell sideways down his chest. "We helped him get the divorce. Then he married Evelyn. They were happy and the marriage seemed good." Quintana stared up at the window.

Rios stood up and paced up and down the row of work tables. "What do you mean seemed good?"

Quintana stood up, stretched. "One never knows about marriage. I mean you could pick a couple you think are ideal in every way, no faults as far as a relationship goes. Then you go and live with them, or you have one take you in their confidence and you find out their life is frustrated by dirty sheets, or poor meals, or someone who snores all night. Perhaps a spouse who is serene and not fun loving, who knows...We thought Evelyn and Ray were happy, and now, well, we hear all kinds of strange things." Quintana shook his head.

"What kind of strange things?"

"No, I can't tell you, I don't know if they are true or just hearsay. Ray was a lonely man, he wanted to laugh and travel. Evelyn never even wanted to go to Jerez let alone travel to Mexico City." Quintana speeded up, his voice slurred.

Rios smiled, he knew the feeling. Marge was a homebody too. "What about Evelyn's sons?"

Quintana sat down, "Evelyn's two sons loved Ray in every way and most important of all Evelyn no longer had to work. Ray won a national award for his kachina dolls and was then asked by the President's council if he would represent the United States in the Indio Exhibition in Mexico City." Quintana grew sad. Rios watched his cigarette glow as he inhaled.

Quintana took a pencil and started to dig down the cuticles on his fingers. "At first he didn't want to go and then Evelyn talked him into it. The United States sent him money and an airplane ticket, hotel reservation notice, and a list of the others who would be traveling with him from this state. There were quite a few from this area, although there weren't too many Ray knew."

Quintana put down the pencil and pushed up his glasses, "Why did he have to die?"

Rios shook his head and walked over to the table where Quintana sat. "Do you know who this is in the photo?" He handed it to Quintana.

Quintana took it, examining it carefully, "No, I don't remember seeing this woman here. Perhaps, well, I don't know, it looks like Alicin's aunt. Yes, this is Grace Ortega. She's a painter from San Thomas Pueblo. She went to Indio. She's all dolled up with make-up and a splashy pink dress. Looks like she's standing next to a man. Who would have ever thought she would do that. She is so shy and modest here." Quintana frowned.

He put the photo down. "You know it was quite an honor for all of us to have Ray go to Indio. It is hard to believe he's dead."

* * * * *

Rios was glad to get out in the fresh air and into his pickup. The sun was going down and the view out his window went to eternity. The land seemed to bend in a curve of earth and mountains glowing with deep red haze. Rios turned and drove into Jerez, the mountains coming up to greet him. Pink clouds on the horizon turned grey, within moments the sun fell over the edge of the earth and the world went dark.

Moses met him at the door. Rios picked up the orange striped tabby cat and stroked him. Moses purred in his arms as they entered. The house was empty.

He walked into the kitchen. A note was on the table, one of the kids had to take their baby to the doctor, so Grandma Marge was babysitting the other two. Rios still couldn't believe they were grandparents. "Well Moses, it's just you and me for dinner tonight."

Saturday, Day 2

The face was wrinkled with time and darkened with wisdom. He was firm about her leaving, and yet there was something that held back. He put her bedroll and duffel bag in the back of the dirty grey truck. The long black and grey braids, wrapped with red yarn, were tucked into his belted breeches.

He opened the door of the old truck and she got in. He walked back into the mud house and came out with a basket, probably to trade in town. He slammed the door shut, then leaned against it, he always did that. He put his hand in his pocket and pulled out the truck keys.

The dogs howled and the truck groaned and lurched out of the dirt driveway. Tears ran down her young face. Her home was moving away from her, moving faster and faster. Now there was only the profile of the Pueblo behind. Fear crept into her throat.

At the gas station no one came out and no one repsonded to Uncle Tito's yell. He stuck his hand through the open window, wrinkled calloused hand hit the horn in the middle of the steering wheel. His hat fell back showing a line of white on his bald head.

Nee-nee pulled her legs under her. Her school dress was thin and the air was cold in the shade. She shivered and peered at Uncle Tito with big brown almond shaped eyes.

This wasn't unusual. There was only one mechanic and he was probably out back with the big machines going and could not hear.

Uncle Tito once told her that no one would ever rob this garage because the man that owned it had an uncle who was a medicine man.

Uncle Tito grumbled and went around the building. He returned with the owner, a big burly fellow with no teeth. He was smiling and slapped Uncle Tito on the back, throwing Uncle Tito forward. Uncle Tito laughed.

"Hi, young lady. Your Uncle tells me you are leaving us. We hardly know you, you are so quiet."

He put the nozzle in the gas tank and produced an old dirty rag for the windshield, smearing colorful oil residue on the scratched glass.

"Where you off to?" The gums glistened in the sunlight. She turned to the side, "I don't know."

The big face smiled, "Well, you must be off to somewhere's 'cause your uncle's not gonna just dump you."

He winked at Uncle Tito. Uncle Tito looked down studying a spot on the truck, rubbing it with his thumb.

Uncle Tito was small compared to the mechanic. On the sides of his head he had round patches of hair down to his waist. He braided his patches into two braids, one on each side of his head. The hat covered his bald spot and gave the appearance of a full head of hair neatly kept in two long braids.

He had soft eyes that spoke in depth without his actually saying anything. Sometimes his eyes were grey and calm, other times sharp blue and angry. Nee-Nee always thought of the stories she was told as a child about Father Sky wrinkling up the Great Up Above when he was sad, and the sky would wrinkle and the thunder would roll out and lightning come down. Uncle Tito had the same wrinkles across his face. He had been a great revolutionary in the Pueblo at one time. Now he kept quiet or found someone else to do the work.

Uncle Tito's clothing was old and worn but his boots were another story. He had traded six of his beautiful baskets for them in Alcala last month. Nee-Nee had taken great care to polish them every night. They were his pride.

He paid the mechanic and got back in the truck.

"See you on your way back. I'll stay open until ten." The mechanic waved and they were off.

"Uncle Tito, where am I going?"

He said nothing.

"Uncle Tito, please tell me where we are going?" He set his jaw and kept driving.

"Is it a secret?" Uncle Tito turned his head and with a soft smile said, "You will know when we get there."

No use in arguing. Nee-Nee stared out the window. He must have a plan. She turned back and studied his face. He was not happy, she could see. She closed her eyes, pulled her thin dress close. The humming of the tires and the sound of wind rattling the seat belt strap against the truck door soon lulled her to sleep.

Uncle Tito touched her arm, his hand cold as ice. She jumped with a start.

"We're here, now you shall have your answers."

She didn't want to be here, wherever it is. He opened the door and she stepped out noticing the road. It was dirt. Uncle Tito's boots were dirty, she smiled. They could get back into the truck and go home, she could get the polish and clean his boots.

"Nee-nee, come on. We are here. Let's go."

He would not desert her. He would not ever.

She walked ahead of him though a thick hand carved wooden gate. The string pull slammed with a bang as it closed behind them. The steps were flagstone, four of them. Down the steps was a fairyland. A tall green willow tree bent to greet them onto a high white portal.

On the south side was the house. It was thick adobe walled with long white window frames that dropped to the floor of the portal. On the north side was a wide green lawn framed with a sea of colored flowers. At the far end was a wooden log fence, grey and old. Straight ahead at the end of the portal along the far west side of the lawn was a path of blooming lilacs ranging from deep purple to soft pastel pink. The end of the lilac path opened to a two story New England red barn with a window high above open double doors. Horses were snorting and kicking the ground under a tall cottonwood tree in the corral near the barn.

Nee-Nee turned her head. She could hear piglets squealing and chickens clucking nearby. Her hand slipped under Uncle Tito's as they stopped in front of a white front door. Four glass panes reflected their stark faces. Uncle Tito pounded on the door.

A tall man answered immediately. "Doc Tapia, this is Nee-Nee." Uncle Tito shoved her forward.

She peered up at the tall man, six feet or more, tan with a Roman nose, dressed in an immaculate suit, expensive. He smelled of Old Spice and leather polish.

Doc Tapia led them into an enormous living room, wall-to-wall grey carpeting overlaid with Persian rugs and old English oak furniture.

"Did you tell Nee-Nee that we expect her to work with us on the farm and we will treat her as if she were one of our own?"

Uncle Tito mumbled, shifted his eyes to the floor and walked outside. Nee-Nee sat quietly on an embroidered couch. Uncle Tito soon pushed open the front door, dropped her things on the hard wood floor of the front entrance room and stomped up the two steps into the living room.

Doc Tapia was staring at her. "Uncle Tito, she is a beauty. The young men must be knocking down your front door to get to her." His eyes followed the outline of her body. Nee-Nee held a frown and her poise, without a flinch.

Uncle Tito mentioned something about Indian blood and then walked over to Nee-Nee. His boots were quiet on the plush Persian rug. She rose to her feet and put her hands out. He pulled a basket from behind him and held his left hand carefully under the basket. He slowly pulled Nee-Nee's fingers under his and pushed them hard against something: a piece of paper.

She followed his eyes, knew she should not say anything. Uncle Tito put his other hand on her wrist; he was shaking. But Nee-Nee felt the strength of his grasp and the tears that were on the verge of coming cleared away. Uncle Tito's soft grey eyes embraced her and his hands dropped. He turned and walked out the door. It slowly closed after him and the catch clicked in place. He was gone.

"Come let me show you to your room. You can put your things away and get comfortable."

Dr. Tapia put his hand into her bent elbow. Nee-Nee hugged the basket, the front facing out. They went down a long hall, passed several rooms that had dark wooden doors, arriving at the room he had chosen. He dropped her duffel bag on the floor next to a canopy bed.

"I shall leave you alone to get used to your room," and disappeared. She could hear his heels echo on the hard brick floor. The echo stopped.

She sat on the bed, her bedroll and duffel bag next to her on the floor. She put her sandal on the duffel bag; her foot on her bag, as her hand lifted long dark hair back away from burning cheeks.

A closet was on the other side of the bed. To the left of it was a light brown mahogany desk for homework, on top a kelly green blotter. In line with the foot of the bed was a window seat inlaid with blue, yellow, and white Mexican tile which framed a double window hung with white lace curtains.

In the corner was a fireplace with a rounded black screen sitting on Mexican tile which matched the window seat. In front of her was a large light brown mahogany dresser with a giant gilded mirror.

On the floor next to the the dresser were high light brown English boots. They were polished and glowing. No wonder Dr. Tapia smelled of leather polish.

A mahogany bedside table with an embroidered white lace doily held a white alarm clock and a brown electric lamp that had once been a kerosene lamp. Her fingers felt the cornflower blue cotton quilted bedspread; the canopy over her head matched.

Why was she here? First try on the boots, decisions later.

* * * * *

The stillness of the night was pierced by the sharp ringing of the phone.

"Yea, what is it?" A sleepy voice answered.

"Sorry to bother you at this hour, but there are fires burning along the river and chanting so loud my family and I can't sleep."

Rios sat up in bed, turned on the light. "Who is this?"

"Sorry, Captain, this is Mr. Hall. We live down from the Mercantile in San Jaime, across from the Church — on the corner by the Hava's. We're on top of the hill going down to the river."

Rios rubbed his eyes, "Does it look like a forest fire?"

"It looks like an anti-war rally. They have torches and drums. The Pueblo itself is quiet, all the lights are out, but looking out my bedroom window at the river, there must be over two hundred people down there."

"Have you been out on the town?"

"Captain, this is fact — something is going on down there and it doesn't look legit. Before calling you I called Cruz and he said not to worry about it. He said we should go back to bed and forget that we saw or heard anything. So I called you, but maybe we should all go back to bed. Good night, Captain Rios," his voice bitter. He hung up.

Rios sat with the phone in his hand. It was two o'clock in the morning. What would two hundred people be doing at the river now. Cruz told Hall to forget it,

What did he mean? Certainly the ZIA would handle any complication that could arise.

He felt a hand on his back, "Is it an emergency or can it wait?" Marge's sleepy voice whispered.

"No, just a bunch of Indians at the river. Mr. Hall says it looks like an anti-war rally."

"There's some fresh tortillas on the counter, do you want me to make you some coffee?"

Rios stood up, "No, get some sleep. Tomorrow little Paola will be here all day, you better rest up."

He dressed quietly and eased out of the front door, yawned, got into the truck. Full moon, cold nights, Indians chanting at the river, and Cruz with strange behavior. Hava's death had started a lot of excitement. He lit a cigarette, pushed back his cowboy hat and started down the road.

Rios drove through the Pueblo. It was quiet. The tall mounds of layered homes ominously loomed in strength, darkness bringing out threatening shadows. Rios rolled the window up, drove by the Hava house. All lights were out. There was only a light on in the Hall's front room, perhaps to ward off any unknown.

Rios coasted down the hill to the river, and turned off his lights. There they were. He could see easily in the light of a full moon. He stopped under a tall cottonwood tree across the river from the torches and fires, and turned off the engine.

He turned on the two-way radio that he kept in the glove compartment: "Carolyn, come in, come in, this is Rios."

There was a crackling and then a sleepy reply, "Yes, Sir, do you know what time it is?"

Rios smiled, "Carolyn, I'm at the base of the bridge at the river on the way to Chima at San Jaime Pueblo. Report and type up the following: Approximately two hundred to three hundred Indians and perhaps Spanish people are here in costumes. They have large fires, four of them about ten feet apart on the Chima side of the river and are dancing in circles and then chasing each other with what appears to be knives or daggers. The men have torches, the shorter people, not sure what sex, have what appear to be skulls. Will report later. Did Cruz call in?"

Carolyn cleared her throat, "Sir, Cruz did not call in. Sir, are you sure that you're seeing all this?"

Rios sighed, "Please type this up and call Carl. I want him to see this."

"Right now?"

"Right now."

Rios turned off the two-way and put it back in the glove compartment, locked it. Anyone could get in there if they wanted to, the truck was so old. Not like Cruz' friends with their fancy brown ZIA cars and all the comforts of a policing unit built in. Rios put his foot up on the dash and pulled out his note-pad, started to draw the costumes.

Suddenly a branch cracked next to the passenger side of the truck. Rios quickly reached down, put his hand on his gun.

"Like the performance? You could join in if you like?"

Cruz and his two ZIA deputy friends were standing outside, their hands on their guns.

Cruz turned his head and spit, "Pretty late at night to be taking in the countryside, ain't it?"

The ZIA deputy got into the truck, his eye caught the glove compartment. Cruz had heard the call over his ZIA friends' two-way radios.

Cruz' tobacco stained teeth glistened in the moonlight, "Not too bright, Captain. I called Carolyn and told her you were loaded on your...well, that you were loaded on your ass and not to bother Carl. Poor girl, she hasn't lost so much sleep in ages."

"Cruz, what in blazes is going on?"

"We'll take you over and show you. You might get a thrill out of it."

Without warning the fat ZIA deputy, whose name Rios couldn't remember, pulled the passenger door wide open and kicked in the glove compartment: the two-way radio crunched with the kick and fell out the bottom. Rios gripped his gun.

Cruz reached quickly, pulled out the keys, throwing them over the truck. "Come on, let's go."

Rios put his foot back up on the battered dash, "Don't think so. I like the view from here much better."

"Let's not get ugly about this. All we want is for you to understand what's going on, Rios."

Rios pushed back his hat, "Are you trying for a promotion, or what? If you are, kicking in that radio is not the way to go about it."

"Come on, enough talk." Cruz pulled Rios out of the truck and sent him flying. Rios landed on all fours and didn't move. He heard Cruz swear at the truck as it started to roll toward the river. Rios reached for his gun, fingers on an empty holster.

"Cruz stop!"

Cruz kicked the back of the old truck as it ground to a stop, it was in gear, Rios didn't have an emergency brake, he always parked in gear. As lights flashed across the road, coming straight in their direction, Rios stood up straight, felt a gun barrel jabbed into his ribs.

It was Carl. He turned to park off the side of the road, picked up a clipboard and pencils, pens, even a recorder.

Carl turned to seek an approving glance from Rios before getting out.

"Captain, why don't you come over here? Oh, hi, Cruz, nice weather we're having for this time year, don't you think?"

Cruz shook his head, "Call him out."

"You call him out. You're the one with the gun."

Cruz pushed Rios towards the car, "Tell him to shut up."

"I'm not moving. You want Carl, you go get him. Or you can shoot me right here."

Cruz signaled to his deputy friend. "Hey, Martinez get over here."

But Martinez didn't hear him. He was too anxious to get back into his fancy car and get out. Cruz yelled out, "Hey, Martinez, damn it get over here!"

Carl started the car. Cruz moved forward standing between the car and Rios. Martinez and the other ZIA deputy ran to their car and backed out, stirring up a whirlwind of dust as they tore onto the road and disappeared into the night.

Cruz pointed the gun at Rios and yelled at Carl, "You stay put."

Headlights on, Carl revved the engine. He was pointed straight at them. Cruz started walking towards the car with the gun pointed at Rios. Cruz walked backwards staring at Carl's car.

Suddenly a hand reached out, grabbed Rios. He felt the tight grip around his upper arm. He was pulled into a group of trees and thrown into the back of a pickup truck. There was no tailgate. The truck rattled, then groaned forward with a lurch.

Rios' arm throbbed, he heard voices all around the truck. He stayed flat, turned his head to the side. He could see smoke coming up from around the truck. They were on the road to Chima, the driver calling out in Indian, waving his hand out the window. Rios could make out the tops of some of the costumes. At last the truck crept up a hill. All was quiet.

Rios lay with his head down. He heard the man inside chuckle. The truck door opened. A hand patted Rios on the shoulder.

"You can get out now. It is safe."

Rios sat up. In front of him was an Indian man painted white, a red bandana around his forehead, colors all over his chest and feathers on a kilted belt. Rios stood and brushed himself off.

"Just dog fur," the Indian laughed. Rios carefully got out of the truck and glanced around.

The Indian man pulled off his bandana and wiped his face, "You were in trouble with a very bad man. He does very bad things here and we are tired of his trouble. I was walking back to my truck after the dance and heard him yelling. So I grabbed you and brought you here. That man in the car, he will know to find you here."

Rios put out his hand, "Thank you, you may have saved my life. You know Cruz, the man with the gun?"

"I know him too well. We all do. He tries to run our lives. I am known as Uncle Tito, you are Dominique Rios and we did not meet here tonight."

He continued to wipe his face. "I have to go home and feed the dogs." Uncle Tito walked over to the truck, pulled on the door, "There was only one person who could get this door open with a gentle touch and now she's gone. That man is bad, stay away."

He backed the truck down the hill, the way they had come. Rios walked to the top. He could see the fires being put out, one at a time. Suddenly headlights turned off the main road and wandered up the hill.

They stopped in the same place as the truck. Rios waited. No one got out. The car was Carl's silver grey Pontiac.

"Captain, if you are there please come on, it's Carl."

Rios stayed. The lights turned off, slid into their compartment in the lower front of the car, light silver grey metal flaps tucking the lights into the car body. Rios still didn't move.

"Captain, it's me. Come on." Carl stuck his head out of the window, looking from side to side.

Then Rios saw someone in the car light a cigarette. Carl was not alone.

Carl slowly pushed the car door open, stepped out into the darkness and hesitated, moving one foot in front of the other, cautiously waiting, then he stopped.

"He's not here. What do you want me to do now?" Carl whispered to the figure in the car.

The figure moved into the driver's seat and the red glow from the cigarette lit Cruz' face. A hand came out of the window, the moon reflected the metal in his hand. Two shots. Carl fell. Rios didn't move. Cruz threw the car into reverse and raced down the hill.

Rios fell on all fours, "Carl, are you all right?"

"Christ, no."

"What was that all about?"

Carl groaned, "Cruz beat me up pretty bad. He wants you. He wants to kill you."

Rios rolled Carl over. There was blood all over his face. He moaned, let out a dull scream and fell back. Rios stood up. "I better get you to the hospital. When I catch up with that son-of-a-bitch there'll be hell to pay."

Rios eased Carl to his feet and lifted him over his back. After stopping several times, Rios finally reached the road and flagged a ride.

"I have a wounded man here, could you help get him to the hospital?" Rios' words were mumbled.

"No problem, Captain, I am Eileen Suazo, a nurse at the Emergency Room. Let's put him in the back seat." She got out of the car and opened the door for him. Rios carefully laid Carl down on his back. He was still, breathing heavily.

"Let's go. Is there a place I can drop you off, or do you need to go in with him?"

"No. You can let me off at the bridge. I'll get my truck and follow you in. Thanks." Rios surprised himself, there were tears in his eyes. He waved as the blue Dodge took off up the hill, through the Pueblo, taking Carl to the hospital.

* * * * *

It was cold outside and working was more than work. Nee-nee called the brown and white spotted cows and shut the long wooden gate to the pasture. Howling barn cats followed her back to the wired chicken coop.

"You are not going to get any squirts of milk now. It is time to bring in the eggs. You go and howl at someone else."

The chickens, mostly hens, had come to appreciate her soft voice. They cackled and moved off the nests for her. One red hen flew down from the roost and landed on her shoulder.

"Oh, you again, how are the ladies? Are they behaving?" The hen pecked at Nee-nee's brown braids.

"I like you too, but I don't pick on you. Least not yet."

She shushed the hen off of her shoulder, held the basket close, and patted the chicken coop door as the cats started howling. With a sudden movement she pushed open the door, howling at the top of her lungs, cats running in all directions. The horses snorted in their stalls and peeked out the trough holes.

Nee-nee walked over to Muster, her favorite. She put the eggs between her feet, reached up and patted his velvet nose.

"Well, I better get back or I'll catch it. You have a good dinner."

Nee-nee ran holding the egg basket high. The lilac path from the barn to the house was always exciting to run through. Nee-nee felt a courageous thrill in her veins as she moved quickly to the house. It was now dark, except for the shadows cast from a full moon.

She pushed the front door open, stamping her feet on the burlap mat. She pulled off her big rubber irrigating boots and tip-toed into the kitchen. Dinner was late again tonight, Doc got home well past eight.

He was on the phone, the frying pan was on the stove, butter burning in it. Nee-nee moved the pan off the flame and put the eggs in the sink, started to wash them.

"Rios, there is only so much I can do. If the orderly stitched up his face, he was following standard procedure. There is not much more I can do."

Doc Tapia pulled out the chair from the long pine dining table and sat down wearily.

"Yes, I know Uncle Tito, but very vaguely, it was at a dance somewhere."

Nee-nee turned her head.

"I can meet you inside an hour at my office. It's locked, so drive around back and I'll meet you there." Doc took off his gold rimmed glasses, grunted a few more times, then hung up. His best form of relaxation was cooking and now he wouldn't be able to.

Nee-nee shook her head. Uncle Tito wouldn't harm anyone or anything, it wasn't his temperament.

Doc Tapia walked over to Nee-nee. "Let me show you how to make a perfect hollandaise sauce."

"Sure," she smiled.

He patted her on the back, "Some other time."

Nee-nee picked up the frying pan and ran cold water on it, steam lifted to her face. The front door slammed shut.

Mrs. Tapia came in the kitchen from the laundry room, "Was that my husband going out?"

"He had just started dinner. He had to go to the office!"

Mrs. Tapia pulled open the refrigerator door. "He was going to fix cold salmon. Perhaps it would be best to save it for Sunday."

"Nee-nee, are you hungry? Is there anything you would like to fix for dinner? Just for a change?"

"It is so cold outside, maybe we could have something like scrambled eggs and bacon."

"That sounds good and a nice change. I'm sure the boys would like that, too. When you were with Uncle Tito did he ever put chili in your eggs?"

Suddenly, Nee-nee's eyes welled with tears. Mrs. Tapia put her arm around her. "Just because you don't live with him anymore doesn't mean you should forget him all together. We should never forget the people that we love. Doctor Tapia has not mentioned him for fear of reminding you of the hard times, but I know you two had some very good times."

Mrs. Tapia always smelled of lilacs. She had long brown hair pulled back in a tight french roll that gave her blue eyes an oriental slant. She was five feet eight with a thin but healthy figure. She worked hard alongside her family, face tanned and hands calloused from work. Nee-nee had always felt there was some Indian in Mrs. Tapia, even though she was from New Jersey. Mrs. Tapia was calm and reserved even when times were tense.

"I miss him, and am so confused as to why I am here."

Mrs. Tapia held her. "I don't know why you're here either, but I'm glad you are. You have been a treasure to us. Let's fix some Uncle Tito eggs, I hear the men coming.

The two sang as they scrambled chili into the eggs. Nee-nee wanted to tell Mrs. Tapia about the phone call, but perhaps she should wait and find out more.

Mrs. Tapia knew Uncle Tito, yet she didn't meet him at a dance. Uncle Tito didn't go to dances unless they were ceremonial dances. Perhaps that's what Doc Tapia meant.

*****

The car lights streaked across Rios' face. He was tired. Even though he and Marge had gone to bed early to reminisce about old times, it seemed ages ago. So many unanswered questions, so many unexpected actions. Doc Tapia parked his dark green Mercedes Benz next to Rios' old pickup. The two men marched to the side door.

"You weren't followed?" inquired Doc glancing around.

Rios shook his head. The doctor opened the door and pushed his way into a sterile white examining room. They walked through the rooms to the office.

It had diplomas covering one side of the wall behind the Doc's desk which filled the middle of the room. It was covered with papers, charts, sample medicines and a tall wooden lamp with a parchment lamp shade.

Doc reached into the bottom of a desk drawer and pulled out a bottle of Cutty Sark.

"You look like a man who could use some medicine. This kind of medicine." Rios eased into a green leather chair, his back and shoulder felt numb, his feet sore. Sitting didn't help and standing hurt. He took the tall glass of brown liquid from Doc's hand.

"What's going on?"

Doc lifted his glass and said, "Cheers." Rios drank, put his glass on the table. "What's going on around here, Doc? You tell me you met Uncle Tito once at a dance. I know he was at your house days ago. You even have a new relative living with you who arrived at the same time or about the same time as Uncle Tito's visit. What happened to the girl staying with Uncle Tito?" Rios shook his head. "I heard all kinds of rumors about the girl. There was even talk that I should go and remove her from such a strange life."

Rios took a drink, liquid burning his throat but warming his temperament. Doc traced the outline of the file on the desk in front of him, said nothing.

"You are avoiding my questions and you probably know more than anyone, you treat the people who come in from the Pueblo. What's going on with Cruz, what is he doing to the people in the Pueblo?"

Doc rubbed the glass between his hands watching the man across from him.

"Doc, I was almost killed tonight, Carl is in the hospital because of a fellow policeman's strange behavior. What is going on? Is this all because of Ray Hava's death?" Rios leaned into the chair, suddenly feeling old and small.

Doc lifted the bottle, filled the glasses again and put the bottle away. He pushed his green leather chair back and placed his eyeglasses on his lap.

"Rios, I'm afraid you've opened up a can of worms. You've gotten yourself right into the thick of it."

Doc rubbed his hand across his forehead. Rios sighed.

Doc leaned forward, "Rios, there is not much I can tell you. A lot of what I know is hearsay and I don't want to lead you astray. There is only one thing I'm sure of, and even that is unscientific and I have no proof. Hava was murdered. He was murdered, somehow, some way, someone got to him. It would have had to be from a distance. Hava's wife was right next to him in bed."

Doc stood up and walked to the deep framed bay window. "Rios, go home and get some sleep. In the morning things will look clearer. Can't imagine what Cruz has against you. He has done some awful things in his lifetime. Hope none of them happen to you."

The Doc turned around. Rios studied him. Doc was worried, his forehead wrinkled. Doc had not answered any of the questions about himself. Did he think Rios would let the mystery of Doc and Uncle Tito slide by?

Rios pulled himself up, "To bed, I should have just stayed there. To put your mind at ease, Carl was attacked by Cruz. Uncle Tito saved my life, perhaps Carl's, too."

Rios walked out the door without turning back. Was he repeating himself?

Sunday, Day 3

Rios stepped out of the shower, dried himself off, pulled on a blue terrycloth robe and stepped into the hall, tripping over the cat as he headed for the kitchen. He fell against the wall.

"Moses, are you after me, too?" Rios grabbed his shoulder. Shooting pains worked up his arm.

"Marge, do we still have some of that deep heating stuff?" Rios picked up the cat and walked into the kitchen. Fresh hot sopapillas lay in a basket on the table. Orange marigolds and purple petunias were stuck in an old glass jar held firmly in Marge's hand, beige phone to her ear in the other. Her soft grey brown eyes studied her husband's face.

"Yes, Carolyn, I will relay the message. Thank you. Did Doctor Tapia find any broken bones?"

Marge put the jar on the stool and pointed to the cupboard over the sink. Rios put Moses down and opened the cupboard door. There was the green medicine he needed. He turned the bottle on its side, the stuff was hard as cement.

"Well, I'll tell Dom to go in around one thirty. Sure...unless the pain stops...all right...the deputies?"

Marge pulled the bottle from Rios' hand, turned on the hot water, and rolled the bottle under it.

"So these men were deputized on a part-time basis...when does the new policeman arrive that was transferred up here?"

Marge drained the hot water out of the sink, turned the bottle upside down, and handed the bottle to Rios. He saluted her with it and left for the bedroom.

"You have met him before? Oh, you haven't..." Marge ended the conversation and hurried to the bedroom. Rios lay on his back trying to rub the medicine on the bruised shoulder.

"How did you manage to carry him so far? He must have been incredibly heavy?"

Rios pulled his robe down to his waist and rolled over onto his side.

"The hardest part was his glasses. I tried to keep them on his nose, they kept falling off. So I put them in his shirt pocket. But once I got him up, they fell on the ground again. So I finally just put them in my pocket...It's strange what you think is so important at the time is really not at all." Rios rubbed his chin. He had shaved too close, his skin hurt.

"Carolyn said that new fellow, Floyd, is coming sometime this week. Also, Cruz' house is still staked out with the part-time deputies and the ZIA Police still will not get involved with the case. Carl has no broken bones, thank God, and is recovering well. She also mentioned you have an appointment with Doc on

Monday." Marge rubbed the medicine deeply into Rios' back and shoulder. "Did you get a chance to talk with Doc last night?"

Rios rolled over and hugged her. "Yes, but he didn't make any sense. Seems like he was trying to protect himself but he just made himself appear more guilty." Rios pulled her on top of him, she leaned her head against his chest. Her hair smelled of soft flowery perfume. He kissed her neck.

Moses jumped on top of her and started purring and digging his claws into her thick blue sweater. Everyone was beginning to feel better.

"Sunday is not a good day for a funeral." Marge took off her wide rimmed black hat, her black dress gave her a youthful glow. Rios paced. Moses sat on the window ledge and watched leaves fall from the tree.

"There is something that won't let me go. It's not that I don't want to, it's just that it doesn't feel right. You were almost killed, no one knows where Cruz is except that he is not at home, and now you want to go and look at a corpse and attend the funeral. It could have been yours."

Marge sank to her knees on the footstool in the living room and burst into tears. Rios shook his head, the frown on his face firmly set, hands shoved into his black overcoat. He put on his Stetson hat, patted Moses on the head and walked out the door.

He started the pickup and rattled off down the road to San Jaime. The wind was up. Tumbleweeds, broken branches, and papers gutted his path as he drove.

The church was surrounded with dark clouds. The people going in were dressed in dark clothing with hats and mantillas. A procession of men carried the coffin into the church.

Rios pulled over and parked next to a red Mercedes. Some class had come to the funeral. Then he saw a woman come out of the Mercantile clutching a brown bag. She got in the Mercedes and drove off. Rios pulled at his coat, fall was brutal.

Uncle Tito met Rios at the church steps. They smiled in passing, separating at the doorway. Uncle Tito was dressed in his ceremonial kilt and leggings, ceremonial paint on his face and arms.

Rios walked over to an empty pew and knelt, said a prayer for Carl, then glanced around. Kneeling in front of him was a woman with a small child, next to her a petite brunette with six children. At the front of the church two pews were filled with Indians dressed in ceremonial costumes. Mrs. Hava was there with her two teenage boys and the Quintana family from the Mercantile.

The smoke from the front altar candles filled the entire church. The priest walked in from the side, his white robe layered with colored silk sashes. The altar was wood with saints and angels leaning forward in heavy abundance. Their eyes were glass or jewels, mouths open, ready to sing or scream.

Rios eased back in the pew as more people filed in. An old man with cuts on the back of his hands sat on the right. He smelled of burnt wood and pinon, his pants were black wool with a dirty brown corduroy jacket and an old blue work shirt.

The man glanced around, leaned over to Rios, and mumbled. "This is the first time I have seen both the Catholics and Indians perform in a church. It is against the will of God."

His yellow teeth smiled at Rios as he pointed a long crooked finger at the Indians. Rios nodded as the Indians moved around the altar.

A large woman with a wide brimmed hat sat down on Rios' left. Her black dress was tight on her mid-section. Her hose had runs up the back, high heels scuffed on the bottom. She knelt in silent prayer then slid back on the pew and opened her purse. She pulled out its contents, a lime green container rolling to the floor. Rios bent down to pick it up, hitting her hat on his way down. The heavy incense odor, dark pews, and solemn mood, mixed with smoke from the candles. "Sorry, " he said as he handed it to her.

She grabbed it and slung it into her purse with the other items. Rios crossed his legs away from the lipstick, blushing powders, and face rouge.

They all stood to sing a hymn. The lady dropped her hymnal; Rios only glanced at her. She reached down, picked it up. The old man shared his hymnal with Rios, his stubbled grin opened and closed to let the sound out. The lady hummed part, sang part of it. Then the benediction, Rios sat back, closed his eyes.

A child behind kept kicking his pew. He sat forward. Something fell behind him, rolled down his back. He turned, picked up a doll with scraggly hair, handed it back to the little girl. She grabbed it from his hand.

The priest talked about Ray and his greatness in the Pueblo. The woman with the rouge started sniffling, tearing, finally she burst into a hard sob, wiping her face on the long sleeve of her black dress. Rios offered his handkerchief. More gracious now, she smiled, took it. Her face was smeared with black mascara, green eyeshadow, red lipstick. Rios watched his white handkerchief slide across the menagerie. He closed his eyes.

The people rose as the coffin was pulled down the aisle. As Rios stood with the congregation, he saw Cruz standing next to the door. Rios counted the people he would have to walk around to get to Cruz. It was not possible.

Cruz would see him and go through the door. Cruz' beard was three or four days along, his cigarette hung in his mouth unlit. He wasn't with anyone but stood with his eyes frozen on the casket.

Several people had to walk around him. He glanced upward, his eyes taking inventory of the church. He did not see Rios. Cruz pulled a lighter from his dirty blue jean pocket.

The Indians in the front of the church began to chant. Cruz shook his head with disgust and disappeared out the door.

Rios moved carefully around the old man, now deep in prayer. He stepped quietly out the side door and was out into the wind.

Cruz was not to be seen. The wind blew a tumbleweed hard against a car. The truck stood alone at the back of the vacant lot next to the Sister's convent.

Rios noticed people were going into the Mercantile. Who would be working and not attending the funeral? Rios pushed the door open. The potbelly stove glowed red with heat, the store almost deserted. Rios shook his head, he thought that Mr. Quintana would close the store for the funeral.

Charles was behind the cash register, the woman with blood red lipstick was cutting up meat. Rios walked over to Charles and asked for a pack of Pall Mall's. He paid for them and went back out into the cold wind.

By now the pall-bearers were coming out of the church. Behind them Indians chanted, dancing around each other. The priest followed the Indians. Perhaps the old man was right. The sky was dark, someone may not approve of this strange mixture of traditions.

The church spewed people: many crying, some solemn, some children were laughing at the Indian dancers. An old woman, bent against the wind playing a Spanish jig on a bent silver harmonica, was the last to exit.

Rios followed the procession to the graveyard. The hole was deep, tumbleweeds in the bottom.

Evelyn stood alone with her sons. There were no tears; her small face was stern, her hands clutching a black purse baring white knuckles.

Rios turned, searching for the woman who still had his handkerchief. She was behind him, to the right. He walked casually to her side. His handkerchief was smeared with color, perhaps he should leave it with her.

As the casket was lifted into the grave, Indian men let out loud yelps and danced around shouting. Rios walked back to the truck, pulled open the door and sat there.

Now people began to enter the Pueblo, some huddled together from the wind. Others were taking off black coats, hats, gloves, and smiling; there was a release of tension now the affair was over. The lady with his handkerchief joined some people she knew, and it became just another item in her purse.

Cars filled with people and pulled out, leaving behind the dark sky and the funeral. Suddenly Rios sat up as he recognized a car in the rear view mirror: a silver grey Pontiac with sleek lines. The front windshield had been punctured with a bullet hole. The car was empty.

Rios lit a cigarette and waited. As the wind buffeted the truck back and forth, he decided to back up next to the Pontiac and find out how empty it might be.

But as Rios started the truck and put it in gear, the Pontiac started also. He still couldn't see anyone inside. Cautiously, he let up on the clutch, the truck moved slowly back. In an instant the Ponitac's engine revved and the car was gone in a cloud of dust.

Rios threw the truck into first and pulled out on the road to follow. A chase was on. Rios smiled, he would catch the Policeman Cruz, and make him eat dirt.

At the interstate Rios could not see a grey car. It had disappeared.

Monday, Day 4

Rios lit his third cigarette. Yes, he was trying to cut down. The office was quiet except for Carolyn's typewriter down the hall. No calls, no interruptions, no word of Cruz. Rios swung his boots off the desk, walked to the door and leaned against it, his hand playing with a fingernail cutter. His eyes examined every crack in the wall — Cruz had something to hide.

Rios ambled to Carolyn's desk, "I'm going. Call me if anything comes up."

Rios started for the stairs, then turned, "Carolyn, did Cruz call you last night?"

Carolyn looked at him, smiled, she didn't hear him. Rios smiled back, reached over pulling the earphones from her head. Her dark red hair fluffed up. He had never noticed the blonde streaks before.

"Carolyn, last night when Cruz called in, what did he say?"

Carolyn pushed her chair back, "It wasn't last night, it was the night before, and he never called in. No, wait, I take that back, the only time I talked to him was when he called about Hava's death."

Rios handed her back the earphones and plodded down the stairs. The sunlight felt good on his shoulder. He reached for the truck door.

"Captain, don't get in, don't open the door. Wait." Carolyn slammed the window down and came running. "Captain, did you have a flat tire this morning?"

"No, has someone been around the truck?"

Carolyn nodded, her green eyes bright with excitement, "When I came to work this morning there were two men working on the tire. Another fellow with long hair and cigarette burns on his shirt was in the truck."

Rios moved around the truck, touching the tires softly. They were new radials he had put on six weeks ago, just paid for.

"I'm glad you remembered to tell me. There's a wire that goes from the driver's door to the dash. Carolyn, let's get Jose from the Motor Division. He would know what to do with this."

"Captain, I left a note on your desk. The men left a bill for repairing the tire. I put it right on top of your desk."

Rios put his hand on her shoulder, "Carolyn, thank you. I may have read it. My mind is preoccupied right now. Please run up and call Jose."

Rios walked over to the back tire and kicked it. Nothing happened. He pushed back his cowboy hat and ran up the stairs.

Carolyn was leaning out of the window to find him. "Jose said not to touch anything, especially the tires. You didn't kick them did you?"

Carolyn pulled the window down. The wind was beginning to pick up. "Jose said to resist the urge — tires are easy to rig with explosives."

Rios frowned, "Who brought up the bill?"

Carolyn led him into his office and handed him the bill from his desk.

"The fellow with the cigarette stains on his shirt was not very nice. He smelled like tobacco and dirt." She picked up her note, threw it in the trash can.

"Captain, the fingerprints you asked for also came in this morning. If you want to look at them, I put them on Carl's desk. The examiner from Alcala said they don't have any of the prints on file, not even Hava's on the account book or the water glass by the bed."

Rios was lost in thought examining the bill as Carolyn went back to work.

Cruz would be dirty. They had his mud shack of a house staked out. But Rios remembered Cruz in a clean new shirt at the church. Maybe his son had gotten it for him, the son that had been brought in twice on charges of selling dope, although they had to let him go for lack of evidence. It always had a way of disappearing.

Cruz had been in the building. Rios opened the bill: Jerry's Texaco, outside of San Jaime Pueblo. It was for a flat tire, but from November the year before. No name, just numbers and a poorly typed address on the back was all Rios could make out. He went over to the coffee maker and mixed two cups of brown flakes, each from a different canister, all poured into a white paper and placed inside the top of the machine. Rios sniffed the mixture, placed a black lid over the white paper's tight trough and then rinsed the clear glass pitcher, wiping it clean with a handful of tissues. Once dried he refilled the pitcher and poured water into a separate trough, holding its lid in his left hand. The mechanized contraption gurgled, rolled with thunder, and began to ooze an amber liquid into another glass pitcher seated on a brown hot plate directly under the white cup concoction. It smelled like malt with a hint of almond and stale barley.

Rios poured a cup once the dribbling ceased. He thought it was strange that Cruz had not set foot in his place of employment for over two years, until now. His check had been mailed out by Carolyn every month. Cruz had never particularly shown like nor dislike towards Rios before. Had the dislike always been there?

Rios called out, "Carolyn, I have a job for you."

"Sir, you said I would never have to go out on police work. That my job was to answer the phone and type orders and reports. Sir, don't make me say no," the freckles on her nose a deep red.

Rios folded a piece of paper and handed it to her. "Carolyn, you were the best in your field at the academy, and now you've decided you want to stay and play it safe. Well, we need all hands now. There's an address on that paper that needs attention. Just drive by the house and get the name off the mailbox, the license number off any cars or other vehicles and report back in. No bullets, no undercover work, very basic stuff, that's all I'm asking."

Carolyn took the paper and stared. Rios folded the bill Cruz had brought,

"Would you please put this in the safe."

Carolyn snatched it from his hand and hurried down the hall. She went down the stairs, the door slammed. She was gone.

Rios sat down at his desk and glanced over the forms on parking downtown, and the review on his request for Carl's new typewriter. An accidental death at the hotel was being brought to court, the family was out for all they could get.

Doc avoided his questions last night. Rios knew Doc was very sharp. And Doc knew Rios would not give up until he had all the answers. What did Doc know of Cruz and Uncle Tito? Perhaps he knew how Hava had been killed and the evidence pointed in Doc's direction. Hava had been killed with some mysterious method. Perhaps chemicals that only one who had knowledge in the field would be aware of. It was far-fetched, but maybe Doc was in on it. Then there was Hava's wife. She was shaken over finding her husband dead in bed with her. Of course all kinds of behaviour surfaces when a murderer has something to hide.

And the young girl at Doc's house was a twist Rios couldn't figure out. She was there for a reason, a purpose. Marge still had her contacts at school, she could find out.

His mind wandered back to Cruz, a man he had known for about five years. He had never thought anything about him one way or the other. They had never had any problems in the past. Cruz managed the Pueblo area quietly, so he never had any reason to distrust him.

He rang up Marge. "Honey, how are you holding up with little Paola?"

Marge laughed, "We've had a great time painting pictures for you. Can you come home for lunch, we made fresh chili?"

Rios sighed, "No, can't make it, just grab something here in town. Marge?"

"Yes..."

"Marge, please lock all the doors and check the windows."

Marge shifted the phone, "Dominique, I have everything closed up tight. Are you all right?"

Rios leaned back in his chair, "I'm a little unsure, that's all. See you later." Rios hung up, sipping his coffee.

Jose was late again. Jose was famous for long lunches mixed with a little cruising down the main street strip. Not much to it, but somehow Jose could spend an entire hour cruising up and down the quarter mile of deserted stores, graffitied stop signs, and faded paint.

Rios called the Motor Division. Jose was on his way. When he hung up he heard the front door slam. Couldn't be Carolyn, she just left.

Rios stood up to call out, then moved away from the desk, the door, and towards his gun on the coat hook. He waited for someone to speak. Steps were coming down the hall to his office. It could be anybody.

"Captain, your truck is a time bomb."

Rios moved forward. Jose jumped. "Man, you could 'a scared me to the grave, man."

Rios smiled, "Just cleaning my gun."

Jose cautiously edged around Rios and the gun. "Captain, that truck of yours is rigged real good. Whoever wired your truck, man, put the explosives on the inside, wired the outside, and split. Real pro job, man. We shouldn't touch it 'til after lunch?"

Rios shook his head, "Jose, I need that truck. I'm Captain of the Police Force. It there is a murder, rape, or accident I have to be there. If it were your sister or mother in trouble, would you want me to wait until after lunch?"

Jose's eyes were round, "Man, if anything happened to my sister I would want you there before it happened, man." Jose frowned with discontent at the thought.

Rios motioned to the door, "Then let's get on with it." Jose limped down the stairs with the Captain bringing up the rear with a flashlight, pliers, wrench, and wirecutters. "Where did you get that limp, Jose?"

Jose pulled his hat around backwards and pushed open the front doors of the station. "Stupid jerk at work, a real dummy, he dumped a car engine on my foot. What a goat, if you know what I mean, it has taken six days for me to be able to walk like a gimp, man. This is some job." Jose pointed to the truck.

Jose held his hand over the window to cut the glare. The reflection in the glass showed Jose's dirty stubbled twenty-six year old face. His nose had been broken numerous times. Grease was wiped unevenly over his pocked face and thick black hair popped out around his stained baseball hat. A button on the back of his hat read, "Do it with grease." Jose was the expert at the Motor Division.

"Hey, man, this job is real messy inside. Let's try the passenger door."

Captain Rios shoved his hands into his blue jean pockets. "I don't think that would be a good idea. I don't want to blow up the old truck, and it could be rigged just like the other side."

Jose stared at him and grunted, "Hey, you think I want my sister raped and have you show up in shorts, no way, man, I'll be careful."

Rios held a smile at that thought. Jose scratched his leg. "The guy who rigged this truck did it from inside, so he must have gotten out and walked away. If he tried to rig the door, it would have been too obvious to the people on the street. Like those watching us now, man."

Jose jerked his head to the side. Rios saw all the store merchants standing on the sidewalk opposite them, talking and milling around.

"Go ahead, pull the door open. If anything it'll be a good show." Rios gazed at the people.

Jose raised his eyebrow, "Hey, Captain, I know what I'm doing, like I'm no dummy, ya know?" Jose pulled open the door. Nothing. Jose smiled then groaned. On the floor was a bundle with six heads of dynamite sticking out. Jose's eyes followed the wire to the driver's door, down the steering wheel where it disappeared under the dash.

"Not a neat job. Dumb guys, another goat at work here. Whoever did this had never been to Nam, man, never took any shop in High School, man."

Jose reached down and cut the wires and pulled them out with a tug. They fell on his feet. "Some dumb goat, man."

Jose then pulled at the wires that went under the dash but they did not come out. He reached down. Rios frowned.

"Another set of dynamite, or a bomb. This dude must really want to blow you up, and the whole town." Jose's eyes glowed, "Now this is more my style, man." Jose pulled off his hat, threw it to Rios. Rios noticed the merchants were moving in closer.

"You better stay back. Jose found a bomb."

They scattered. "Hey, Captain, you must have found a lead on the Mafia," Mr. Gabaldon the butcher yelled. Rios waved.

Jose's feet swam in the air as his head dived under the dash. "Hey, man, could you hand me the flashlight and we better get the tool box for this." Jose pushed his hand into the open air.

In his hand was a crumpled note. It fell to the ground as Rios handed Jose the tool box. Rios picked it up with dread and read the scribbled long hand:
YOU LEAVE SAN JAIME ALONE OR YOU WILL
FOLLOW HAVA TO THE GRAVE

Rios grinned, rubbed his chin. Threats were not to be taken lightly, and threats were not to be given lightly either, especially to a policeman from a policeman.

Jose grunted and groaned, pushed and pulled, mumbling something about lunch. He finally emerged.

"Hey, man, if this thing blows up on top of me bury me with it." Jose disappeared again, under the truck this time. An hour passed.

Rios leaned against the truck, lost in thought. If Cruz did this then he must be desperate. Rios was still puzzled about Cruz after he shot Carl. Cruz may have killed Hava, but for what reason? They did not travel in the same circles. Cruz was more the beat-up-and-shoot-ask-questions-later type. And Hava had been killed secretively with a great deal of forethought, not like Carl's brutal treatment.

Rios tipped his hat to Mrs. Tipton. Her husband ran the newspaper. Mr. Tipton would be a good man to talk to, he should have the history on Cruz over the last couple of years. The bells from the church struck the hour.

Jose moved out from underneath the truck, "There, fixed it. I know who's work this is, it's the same goat that worked in the Motor Division. Wonder who he's working for now. This is my wire, and under the main shaft was my screwdriver I lost the week he was at Motor Division." Jose handed the screwdriver to Rios. It was bent and flattened. "The truck had the brakes cut and the gas tank has a hole in it. The bomb is defused. You can drive it, man." Jose wiped his brow, took his hat from Rios, flinging it on his head. "I gotta eat, man. See you Captain." Jose walked off.

"Jose, wait up. Why don't you let me give you a lift back to your car?"

Jose pulled his hat on, "No way, man, thanks anyway." Jose without turning waved his hand in the air. Rios went over and kicked the back tire. It was solid, he could drive it.

Rios opened the door of the driver's side and slid in. The engine started up, no explosion. He pushed it into gear. The truck started to roll, he pushed on the brakes, "No brakes." He eased his way to the Texaco station down the street.

The truck's age came out once it was lifted into the air. The underneath looked like a dead long-forgotten dinosaur skeleton. It was corroded, rusty, years of mud and dirt hanging from the axle. Max put on his mining hat, his hands black with grease and dirt. The tires hung in mid-air gaping at the ground.

"Wair's ya off ta and ha long ya be gone?" Max pushed the wrench into a red drawer. Rios sighed, "I thought I could wait here. I have a doctor's appointment at one-thirty."

Max shook his head, "Danna look like eet be done by den. Ya half a ride ta get ya dere?" Rios listened intently, he couldn't guess where Max was from. When asked, Max would shake his head and change the subject.

"No, I don't have another ride. Do you have a truck I could borrow?" Rios pushed his hat back.

Max gave him a funny look, "Ya be on the careful wid it, tho, for ya been ruff wid da druck we gots here." Rios nodded. "I'll be careful."

Max threw him a set of keys. "Da only one dat runs in da mud around here is da blue druck offer dere." Max lifted his hat back, the long red hair fell to his shoulders. Max pointed a long greasy finger to a blue truck with a For Sale sign on it. Rios waved to Max. He slid into the driver's seat and drove to Doc's.

The parking lot was full. If Doc had this many patients in his office, Rios would be waiting all day. He parked the truck near the end of the lot, pushing down hard on the emergency brake. It didn't work. Rios threw the truck into first.

The day was warm, the wind slight, the sun heating up the earth. The large wooden door was cracking with age. Rios yanked it open. You couldn't be too sick or you would never get this door open to see the Doc.

Rios had always come in the back way before. Now the room was glazed with smoke and full of people milling around. Phones were ringing, women talking, children crying, old people coughing. Rios blinked. He walked over the toys, around the feet, through the misplaced chairs, to the secretary.

She put the phone down, glared up at him. "There's another one here, Karen." She threw a brown medical chart to the nurse behind her.

"Yes, who are you, when is your appointment, and have you seen the Doc before?" She heaved in her chair. Her thin build, small bust, white uniform, fluffy hair-do all moved at the same time. Rios took his hat off.

"Yes, I have been here before. I am Captain Dominique Rios and my appointment is for one-thirty."

The secretary smiled, "Maybe you will get in by then. Let me look for your chart again. I didn't find it earlier. When were you here last?"

She stood up. Her perfume was sweet. "Captain, were you here to see the Doc as a patient?"

Rios smiled, "No, I haven't seen Doc as a patient for many years."

The secretary sat back down with a frown. "Then you will have to fill one of these out." She pushed a clipboard toward him. "Then we will know all your secrets."

Rios read the questions. "Would you please find a seat and fill it out. There are some people behind you." Rios turned avoiding a pregnant woman with two children.

"Excuse me." He walked over to the corner of the room, filled out the form, stepped back across the feet, handed it to her. "Don't sit down, you're next." She pointed to a white door.

Florence, the Doc's nurse met him on the other side. "Hi, Rios, come with me." She led him down the hall to a vacant room.

"Strip down to your shorts, I'll be back in a moment." She closed the door. Rios put his hat on the chair in the corner of the small room. The floor was tiled, the examining table covered with white paper. The Doc's diplomas (some of the many) were hanging on the wall. One had dirty fingerprints on it. Rios sat on a chair. It creaked, tilted to one side, but held his weight.

Guarding the instability of the chair, Rios pulled off his boots. His socks had holes. They were his favorites, they deserved to have holes. He quickly stuffed them inside his boots, the nurse wouldn't notice. Rios unbuttoned his shirt, listening to the hall noises. An older woman couldn't manage to put anything into the little bottle, a child was going to the hospital for x-rays.

Rios' toes curled at the cold floor acquaintance. The t-shirt was new, maybe he could leave that on. The heater next to the chair went on, blasting hot air on his legs. Rios moved the boots away from the heater and hung his shirt up on the back of the chair. His belt buckle was a gift on his wedding day. The silver still shone, mostly from wear. Marge thought it was the best present they got. Rios pulled the buckle loose, let it fall. He unbuttoned his jeans.

There was a knock at the door, Florence stepped in. "Captain, you're going to have to strip down. I'll wait outside for a few minutes, then we will need to get your weight and height." She stepped out, closed the door.

Rios looked at his naked toes, unzipped his pants, let them fall. He sat down on the chair and pulled them off. The nurse came back.

"Please take off your t-shirt." Rios pulled it off over his head. The t-shirt made the difference, he was now twelve years old.

Doc walked in while she was weighing him. He had his reading glasses on. He studied Rios from head to foot. Rios frowned.

Doc mumbled, sat down on the chair. He sat down on top of Rios' blue jeans. The chair tilted. The nurse pulled the rumpled paper off the examining table, asked Rios to sit on the table.

Rios' feet touched the cold floor again. Doc wrote something on the chart, stood up and patted Rios on the back.

"Shoulder still sore, huh?"

The nurse gave Rios a cutting glance and walked out. Florence had dated Carl for two years but something happened and they stopped seeing each other.

Doc twisted Rios' neck until he almost broke it and thumped him on the back. He held a lighted device in front of Rios' eyes, studied Rios' nose, then his ears. The cold stethoscope moved on the belly, on the back, and at last on his chest. Doc scratched his head, sat down and wrote on the white paper.

"Well, what do you think is wrong with my shoulder?" Doc continued to write. "Is it a pulled muscle?"

No answer. Rios leaned over and pulled his t-shirt from the chair and over his head. "I'm going to give you this for rest. Those muscles are tight. Fill this right away and take only at night. It has a pain reliever in it." Doc patted Rios on the shoulder and disappeared out the door.

Rios stood up and got dressed. The nurse did not come back. He listened to the sounds in the hall, opened the door and walked out into the crowded passage of people.

* * * * *

At lunch Debbie sat with Gerald and Nee-nee went over to talk with them. She pulled down her long black braids to her waist, "Hello, Debbie. I came to say you needn't bother to ask Gerald about what happened in the Pueblo because I already know."

Debbie stared into her food. Gerald stood up, "You know what?" Nee-nee stood very straight, "I know what happened in the Pueblo yesterday, and last night." Gerald took Nee-nee by the arm and pulled her down into a cafeteria chair. "Nee-nee, I don't know what you know and I don't care. But if you keep spouting your mouth off about what you know you may end up with no mouth."

Gerald turned and looked around him.

His eyes stopped, "See that tall Indian kid with the braids and the feather?"
Nee-nee nodded. "He's Cruz's spy."

Nee-nee shrugged, "So . . ."

Gerald winced, "So . . . is that all you can say? Don't you know who Cruz is?"

"So, I never met him, is that a sin. Why should I care who he is?"

"I can't believe it. You lived all of these years in the Pueblo and you never met up with Cruz?"

"No, I never met him."

Gerald spoke under his breath, "We all keep bumping into him from all sides. Uncle Tito must hold something over on him if you never met Cruz."

Nee-nee started to stand.

Gerald stood up with her, "It would make things a lot easier if you were scared. You should be. Nee-nee, just be careful what you say. You could end up dead."

Debbie pushed her chair back. "Gerald, aren't you getting a little too excited about this?"

Gerald glared at her. "No, strange things have been happening in the Pueblo which big mouth here could not know anything about. Fatal things, and to too many people without reason. I think we better not talk about it anymore."

Nee-nee turned slowly and walked outside. Gerald said fatal. Could he mean like his stepfather dying? Nee-nee sat down and waited for the bell to ring.

Alex, the kid with the braids and feathers, came out of the cafeteria with a bunch of tough guys. Nee-nee thought she saw him giving her the once over with his eyes. The bell rang. Uncle Tito could be in trouble. Perhaps it was time for her to go home now. She would ask Mrs. Tapia.

Nee-nee gathered up her books from her locker. Debbie bumped into her, "You really upset Gerald. Perhaps we had better stay apart for a while." Nee-nee's eyes welled with tears. Debbie pushed her way out into the crowded hall. Nee-nee slammed the locker shut.

"You in a hurry, or can we talk?" It was the guy who was supposed to be Cruz's spy.

She glared at him, "What do you want?"

He smiled showing cracked front teeth, "I am Alex Cruz, and you, what's your name?"

Nee-nee let the pulsating flow of students pushing down the hall move her toward the doors. "Why?" She said, turning her head.

"You're kinda cute."

Nee-nee laughed. Dan was moving towards her. She grabbed him by the arm and yelled back to Alex, "Thanks, I needed that." She let Dan push the way to open air.

"What was that all about?" Dan asked, patting her clenched fingers wrapped in a hard grip around his upper arm.

"Who knows, but I think I better be careful around that guy. He's spooky." They ran to the bus. Nee-nee didn't look back.

* * * * *

Rios walked down the aisles of toothpaste and toilet paper. The pharmacist was on the telephone. Rios noticed that the counter was up to his shoulders and the small woman standing in front couldn't see the pharmacist at all. Rios shifted his weight. His shoulder throbbed.

"Yes, who is next?"

The small woman reached up into the air, flinging her prescription over her head. A thick fingered hand grabbed it up.

"Just have a seat, it'll be about ten minutes." The pharmacist shoved the medical paper onto a clip board. He glanced at Rios.

"Ah, yes, the honorable Captain of the Police Force has arrived for his prescription. Doc called it in so if you had an emergency, you wouldn't have to wait."

The pharmacist smirked behind thick mirrored glasses. He walked behind the shelves, pounding heels into the clean white linoleum floor and disappeared into the back. Rios heard a door slam.

The woman started to sneeze. Rios read the labels on the medications shelved in front of him. There were four different kinds of Vitamin E, several kinds of eye cleanser, a dozen kinds of condoms.

Rios smiled. He remembered how difficult they were to come by when he was a kid. All the boys thought it was important to carry one in their wallet. They would take them out at baseball games and compare styles.

Footsteps came towards Rios. "Here you go, now the Doc said you should only take these at night. However, if the pain becomes extreme, just take one with coffee." He handed the bottle to Rios.

Rios watched his reflection in the pharmacist's glasses. He could not remember ever seeing George Gundrall's eyes. The man had been a pharmacist for years and it bothered Rios that he could not remember ever seeing the man's eyes. The eyes are a reflection of the soul. The pharmacist waited until he left before starting the next prescription.

Rios walked to the checkout stand. He could feel someone watching him. Maybe it was his imagination, or maybe not.

Mr. Romero was arguing with his wife. "You always buy the same permanent stuff. Then you go home and fix your hair, and then you go to the beauty parlor and pay thirty dollars to get it all cut out. Why not save us some money. Just put it back."

Mrs. Romero smiled at Rios, "Are you not feeling well?"

Rios grunted, "Sore shoulder. It just acts up whenever the weather is bad."

Mrs. Romero pressed her fat stomach into his side, 'I would not get anything filled here. I go to Alcala for our prescriptions. Did you hear about what happened last year to the Davis' poor sweet child?"

Rios put his boot against the gumstand, "No." He knew she was determined to tell him.

"Well this pharmacist, Mr. Gumdrill, or Gundrall, or whatever, gave them, the Davises, the wrong prescription for their sweet little boy. The Doc ordered a certain kind of medication and the pharmacist was out of it. So he gave them another drug that the boy was allergic to or something. He put the name of the drug the Doc wrote on the bottle, but he put a different kind of drug inside the bottle."

Mrs. Romero stopped to catch her breath, "They went back East and the next thing they knew their little boy was not breathing right. They took him to the hospital and the boy almost died. Now he is alive, but the sweet thing is suffering from brain damage. Mala suerte if you ask me. Que feo." She wiped a tear away.

Mr. Romero pulled her away, "Lousia, don't scare the Captain."

"Well someone is trying to kill the Captain. Why not that evil man?" She jerked her chin towards the back of the store.

Mr. Romero showed his teeth to Rios, "Please forgive her. She watches too much TV. Que bruja."

Rios nodded. He waited for them to finish and then paid for his medication. He popped one in his mouth and jumped into the truck. The gelatin capsule stuck in his throat. He coughed it up, threw his head back and swallowed it again. Down it went.

Rios glanced behind him at the traffic. Two cars were backing out. This parking lot had an average of four accidents a week. Mrs. Tipton's blue Thunderbird pulled up and let the old Volkswagon that the Romeros were in go first. Rios turned and faced the front, glancing in his rear view mirror.

Mrs. Hava walked out of the drugstore carrying a large bag. Suddenly, a tall man with a little girl bumped into her. She lost her balance and dropped the bag. Rios started to get out and help her, then stopped.

The big man, a tourist, picked up the bag and handed it to her. The bottom ripped and bottles of prescriptions rolled onto the sidewalk. Each bottle had a label neatly typed, as far as Rios could tell. Rios leaned back. His shoulder still throbbed.

A woman came out of the store, Sylvia, the checkout lady, and helped Mrs. Hava put the things into a new bag. Mrs. Hava reached down into the torn bag and pulled out a large square box of photography paper. Rios backed up and drove back to the police station.

"Carl, what we need is a good lead on the people who were with Ray Hava the day before he died." Rios walked around the desk. "Now that Tim has moved to Alcala, it is just you and me. So where do we start?"

Carl pulled his pipe from his pocket. "Well, how about San Thomas. Maybe I can find that Grace. She may know what was going on in Ray's thoughts. She went to Indio with him. Or on one of their nights out in Mexico City, he let something slip." Carl lit his pipe, filling the room with heavy smoke.

Carl's face was still in delicate condition. The beating left bruises that were slow healing on his chin and left cheek and his left eye had a sleepy droop.

"All right, you go and check out San Thomas. I'm going to the newspaper and find out all I can on Hava and Cruz. Do you know anything about Cruz before he came here?"

Carl turned his back to Rios and relit his pipe. "All I know is that one time before he beat me up he called me to San Jaime and asked me if I knew anything about cameras. I told him I had a darkroom and he wanted to know if I had any special paper that you can use to develop negatives on. I told him yes. He asked me to bring it out to the Pueblo, so I did. Only it was very strange. He wanted to meet me down by the river. So I obliged the fellow. Then when he took the paper, he beat me up."

Rios fell into his chair. "Why didn't you tell me about it?"

"Well, Uncle Tito came along and got into an argument with Cruz. It almost came to blows. Cruz went over and pulled my car keys and threw them into the trees. But Uncle Tito just took my arm, put me in his truck, and drove me up the hill."

Carl smiled, "Later, I came back and got my keys and drove home. Cruz avoided me after that. But he sent me a check for the paper. It bounced, so I tore it up."

Carl put his pipe in his pocket. "Is there any news on my car?" He almost whispered.

Rios frowned, "It's been seen, but we can't stop the car long enough to find out who has it." He had said 'we' instead of 'I', hoping Carl wouldn't notice.

Carl pulled the pipe out of his pocket and shoved it into his mouth. His teeth clenched over it, "They better not hurt my baby. Cruz probably has it. Can the Police Department rent a car for me?"

Rios called the garage. They would bring a car for Carl directly, filled with enough gas to get him to San Thomas and back. Carl thanked Rios and went down to meet them.

Meanwhile, Rios pulled Cruz's file off the pile on his desk. He opened it, studying dates, names, and places. Cruz had been around, but never in one place long, although he had always come home to San Jaime. The last job was at a diner in Square Corners. He had declared bankruptcy and cleaned up the town.

Rios walked down the hall to Carolyn's desk. "Oh, boss, this says Carl's bills will be put through the Police Station for his medical expenses. How do we do that?"

Rios glanced in her direction, "Send it to bookkeeping."

"But I'm the bookkeeper."

Rios tipped his hat, walked around her down the black stairs and out the heavy metal door.

Carolyn stood up, pushing her thin body against the railing. "Hey, when can I tell you about the address you sent me to find?"

"When I get back." The door slammed.

Mrs. Tipton had limited information. Cruz was only mentioned once in the last five years. Ray Hava had been written up for each one of his trips. The society page was full of descriptive information. Hava was a famous Indian. But the obituary was a brief description of his life. Ray Hava had served his purpose.

"Did you find what you're looking for?" Mr. Tipton came forward, apron covered with ink hanging down to his pant legs.

"Yes. Did you know Cruz beat Carl up the other night?" Rios handed Tipton the bulk of the papers.

"We heard about it. We thought it would be best to keep it quiet. Not too good for the police force if we have them trying to kill each other in print."

Tipton wiped the ink off of his fingers. "Would you like some coffee?" Rios followed him into the next room.

"We were not surprised about the incident. Cruz is a well known trouble maker. He's tried to get us to print things but we flatly refused. He wanted us to do a number on Hava. Print about his marriages, and the ladies he met in strange places."

Tipton handed Rios a mug of coffee. The aroma wafted up to Rios' special senses.

"It was a scam job, as we call it. He wasn't fond of Hava for some reason. He threatened to expose us if we didn't go with his wishes, shady wishes." Tipton put his head back and laughed. "We told him to go right ahead. Do you know what he did then?"

Rios pushed his hat back, savoring the coffee flavor. South American coffee freshly ground brought Rios to life.

"Cruz brought in a photo of my wife and I hugging each other in front of Roybal's store." Tipton talked louder. "It was the day our first grandson was born. We were hugging each other all day long. Can you imagine that?" Tipton started to giggle, shaking his head and tapping his brown tipped shoes. "As if that photo could harm anybody."

Rios finished his coffee. His smile was not only for the comedy of Cruz's threat, but for the good coffee. Rios pushed out into the strong wind. Signs of a sale were pasted in the windows of the Jerez Drugstore. Rios peered in through the windows to find Sylvia peering back at him. He glanced quickly at the flower store. They had a large bouquet of daisies in the window, white and yellow. Mrs. Guiterrez was sweeping the floor. She raised a smile to Rios.

Rios walked across the street to the hardware store. Three trucks were out in front, one man was loading up large burlap sacks of grain. Probably a sale item, the cold winter wind was moving in. Rios noticed the cracking sidewalks. Their new mayor was going to take care of them, as well as the potholes in the main street.

The station was straight ahead, a two story building new to the town. It rose above the older duller buildings. It was painted off-white with green window frames. The first floor was never finished. It gave the appearance of being enclosed from the front but when seen from behind, the first floor was just an empty shell. Next summer it was to be finished. Rios would then be able to have a full staff.

Now it was just Carl, Cruz, Carolyn and himself. Cruz was out and there was another man, Floyd Custer, about to arrive any time now. He wanted to move up to this quiet little town from Houston. He was a rookie cop with a love for the outdoors.

Rios pushed the big doors open and went up the stairs. "Any calls?" Carolyn shoved in the file drawer. "No, should there be?"

Rios smiled, "If the man from the Dairy Queen calls and still wants to know if the car that was smashed in his lot will be towed away, tell him he'll have to pay for it." Rios walked down the hall.

"What about my reports?" Carolyn called after him.

"I have to talk to Mrs. Hava, leave them on my desk."

* * * * *

Carl drove west, his rental car leaving a long trail of billowing dust behind him. The sun reflected off of his thick glasses. His smoke trailed out the driver's window to mingle with the dust outside. The radio clamored out an old love song from the fifties. Carl hummed along.

The long winding road turned into a sharp bend, curved down over a bridge and dropped into a well used arroyo. The car groaned in the sand.

"You would think these rich Indians could afford a better road." Carl steered away from a cow and her calf, going up the embankment. He pulled in front of an adobe building.

Carl closed the door and reached through the open window to pull out his clipboard, note pad and pocket case filled with pens. His pipe was pushed into his blue jean pocket, the bulge giving a noticeable difference to his shape. He walked into the ZIA office.

"Do you know where I might be able to find Grace Ortega?" A short round Indian woman behind the desk pushed her embroidery under a telephone book, "Who?"

"Grace Ortega?"

The woman pushed through the pages of the telephone directory, Carl turned, stomped to the door and stood there listening as the woman called Grace Ortega on the phone.

"She wants to know who you are?"

Carl slouched his shoulders, reached into his blue jean back pocket and produced his Police I.D. and placed it in the chubby brown hand. She read his name off the card. It was the only thing he understood for she was mixing his name with her native tongue.

"Hokay, she will see you. Do you know San Thomas?" She studied the bruises and hurts on Carl's face.

Carl shook his head.

"Drive to the end of the dirt road on this side of the building until you come to a house with a red gate and blue shutters." She pointed behind her to the west.

"Thanks."

The red gate was surrounded with mutts. Carl brought his cane this time. Since he had it, might as well use it. The dogs all backed away when he pushed open the gate.

Carl reached up to knock on the door. It was mostly glass. A woman inside motioned him to come in.

Carl walked into the room. There was a fire in the corner, a neat table with a checkered table cloth, and the best of smells.

"Come in. May I take your coat?" The woman was small with delicate features. Her hair was braided tightly around her head several times and she wore a blue paisley dress with a light brown apron.

Carl thought she could have stepped out of a storybook picture. He sat down, she offered him coffee. She had a hearty laugh, and spoke without an accent. "Hava knew how to pick his women," Carl thought to himself.

"It is good of you to let me come and talk to you. As you know, Ray Hava is dead. The Captain and the Doc feel there was foul play involved. Could you answer some questions about your trip to Mexico City and the Indio fair?"

Grace held her breath, then nodded. Carl pulled out his clipboard.

"When did you first meet Ray Hava?" He sat abruptly on a banco.

Grace smiled, "It was at the Gallup Ceremonials about four years ago. His booth was next to my husband's. My Joe was showing his jewelry."

Carl wrote on his clipboard.

"Mr., would you like some coffee?" Carl hurriedly answered, "Yes." Grace Ortega went quietly into the kitchen.

Carl glanced around the room. The couch was covered with a fine thick red Navajo blanket. The walls were hung with large Indian paintings, on each corner of the paintings hung feathers. The table had a cup of coffee sitting on it, bills, and a photo album. The photos were turned upside down. Carl heard Grace Ortega talking to someone, no, she must be on the phone.

"I hope you like homemade cookies?" She set a tray on the table in front of him. The coffee was steaming. Carl asked her about the hotel where they had stayed in Mexico City, and the Fair itself. Carl realized his approach was too direct for her, his head was moving too fast for his thoughts to be diplomatic.

Her answers were definite and to the point, but she didn't tell very much. Carl was almost surprised that she even considered answering them. She continued as though it was her duty to tell him what he wanted her to say, without telling him anything at all about herself or the relationship she may have had with the dead kachina man.

She had seen Ray several times, they ate at different tables, they were involved in different time classes, for they were involved in two different types of Indian art. She had gone for a stroll with him on the last day, but there were eight other people. She had a list of their names if he wanted.

Carl realized she was guarding herself, waiting for something to happen. The glass window in the door was her focus of attention. She was clever and he was the cop. Carl drained the last drop of coffee from his cup as a truck drove up and the dogs started to bark. Grace jumped and went to the door.

Their voices were low. She went outside and spoke quickly. The ground moved with their entrance. Cups rattled as they stepped into the house. Carl held his breath. His bones groaned as he realized how vulnerable he was.

There were six tall men. The thinnest appeared to weigh about three hundred pounds. Corn husks flopped in their hair which was powdered with ash. The immense bodies were coated with red mud. They had on leather loin cloths that barely covered their loin area. The thong aroung their middle pulled on the bulging protrusion of their bellies. They filled the entire room. Their eyes were circled with black paint, mouths smeared with grey matter. The odor and the immenseness of the six dominated every space. Huge dirty feet pointed at Carl.

The heaviest approached Carl. He took the clipboard, broke it across his knee.

The crack echoed through the room, through the house, and through Carl's mind. Carl's whole being started to throb. The biggest man took Carl by the arm and led him out of the house. Outside there were four more, these had rifles.

Carl did not resist.

One of the men got into Carl's car, the driver's seat. The man who had Carl's arm stuck his hand out. Carl put his fingers into his pocket, rustling though the pipes, tobacco, change, and rabbit's foot for his keys. He dropped them into the man's hand. Another of the group got into the passenger's side of the car. The car dropped two inches closer to the ground.

Carl was pulled into their truck, into the middle of the front seat. The man grunted to the driver, waved to Grace, and got in beside Carl. Carl had loaded rifles on either side of him.

Grace Ortega had called for help, a call for the Big Men. Carl lifted his arms in closer to his body, a piece of bologna between two pieces of whole wheat Indian bread. The men in Carl's car drove ahead of them. It almost bottomed out going over the embankment of the arroyo.

The man sitting next to Carl pointed to a sign by the road. It read:

NO NOTE TAKING
NO TAPE RECORDING
NO PHOTOS TAKEN
ABSOLUTELY NO CAMERAS

Carl had broken several of these rules. But he was a police officer, although he certainly wasn't going to bring it up. The car stopped at the main highway. Carl was pulled out and pushed to his car. The others got out leaving the driver's side open.

"Don't come back, you, or you may never leave again," one man mumbled holding his rifle up pointed at Carl.

"I won't." Carl jumped in and drove up onto the interstate. "Wait until Rios hears about this." Carl raised his hand to the sky.

He drove into the parking lot, grabbed the paper notebook off the seat and bounded up the stairs.

"Where's Rios?"

Carolyn put her hand up and breathed into the phone, "Yes, Sir, I have told him about it. We will remove the car as soon as it has been approved in Alcala. No, Sir, I don't know how long it will take. It could be this afternoon. All right, well, that's all I can tell you."

Carolyn hung up, "What a temper. Rios is in San Jaime talking with Mrs. Hava. What in the world happened to you. There's dirt all over the seat of your pants."

Carl smirked, "You can type my report. I'm going to dictate it now."

Carolyn frowned, "Oh, joy!"

* * * * *

Rios stopped the truck and opened the large creaky door. It swung back and almost caught his leg. Rios held still and watched it thud against his boot. He had never had problems with the door before.

He walked up the hill to Hava's house, the ground rolling in front of him. His boots pulled his legs up and over the humps of dirt. Rios' long fingers reached up to the door and knocked.

"Yes, oh, Captain. I was expecting you. Please come in." Her face was soft and dripped down into her deep brown velvetine blouse. Rios followed her into the front room.

"Would you like another look around?" Her voice was soft. Rios' head moved back and forth, stopped and changed into a nod. His head took a long time to stop. The clock in front of him smiled and pointed its long finger to the bedroom.

"The bedroom is where I would like to begin."

Mrs. Hava stood aside. Rios rubbed his eyes, putting his dark glasses away. His eyes blurred with images. He tried to focus and gain control of what he was seeing, but something blocked him from thinking clearly.

The step down almost broke his neck. His foot had forgotten to hold him up. Rios reached for his head. He moved over to the bed and sat down.

"Can I get you something, Captain, you don't look well."

"Would you have any coffee, or orange juice?" Mrs. Hava smiled, "You may be coming down with the flu. Even police officers can get sick." She blurred off into the darkness.

Rios dug his fingers into the bedspread. He was not going to fall over on this bed. A man died in this room, on this bed. Does she still sleep here after what happened? Death bed, get off of the death bed.

Rios leaned forward and stood up. The bottle of pills from the pharmacy fell to the floor. Rios heaved his body forward to pick the bottle up, his body rigid.

"Let me get those for you. Why don't we go into the kitchen. It is a lot brighter there and we can sit and talk." She picked up the bottle and pushed it into his shirt pocket. She took him by the arm and led him up the step, through the front room, down a hall and into a bright kitchen. Rios covered his eyes. The light burned his face.

"I think I should go," Rios' knees were weak under him. The words slurred from his mouth.

Mrs. Hava pulled a chair out for him. "Here, I will close the shutters. Sit down a moment and have some orange juice and coffee. If you still feel poorly, my boy will drive you into town." She pulled the shutters closed. The room came in to focus. The orange juice cleared his left eye, the coffee cleared his right.

"Did Doc give you those pills? Perhaps you should take one and you might feel better." She pointed to his pocket with a long delicate finger that almost went through him.

Rios picked out the bottle and pried the lid off. He swallowed one large pill. Rios asked her about her gingham blue curtains, had she sewed them herself. They talked for awhile, although Rios wasn't sure of what. His head felt fuller.

"Thank you for the refreshments. I feel better now. Please let me know if Cruz tries to contact you, or if his son threatens your boys again." Rios waved as he walked to the truck. People floated past him going in and out of the Mercantile.

Rios could envision Hava lying on his bed dead, with no hope of ever waking up. That man would never walk to the Mercantile again.

The old truck banged its way back to the Police Department and Rios sat there with the motor off. Carl was back with two cars. The rental car and his grey Pontiac were parked in front of the door.

Rios put one boot down on the stairway, then the next boot on the next stair. He could never remember doing this before. He must have. This was the only way to his office. This would pass.

Carolyn was on the phone as he glided to her desk. Her red hair shot lights of red and gold. Rios blinked and took off his sun glasses. The light was too bright, he fumbled for them in desperation and got them back over his eyes.

"Captain, am I glad to see you." Carl came out of his lab room. "San Thomas still has Mud Men."

"Mud men here?" The words appeared.

Carl stepped beside him, "No, not here, at San Thomas. They gave me an escort out of the Pueblo. You know the sign that says "No note taking." well, I blew it. I was taking notes. So they escorted me out of the Pueblo with rifles."

Riso shook his head, "You're going too fast for me. Let me sit down."

Carl led Rios to his office and pushed the windows open to let in fresh air. The light from the windows burned Rios' face. He winced.

"Dom, are you all right? You look white as a sheet." Carl shut the windows and pulled the white curtains across the blinding light.

"Carl, could you get me some water? My mouth is dry. Maybe I should take another of Doc's pills. It helped before."

Carl poured some cold water from the turned off coffee maker into Rios' coffee mug. "Here. Where are your pills?"

Rios let his knees buckle under him, the chair was hard. "Here." Rios plucked them out of his shirt pocket. Carl tried to get the lid open.

Rios grabbed the bottle and pushed down hard on the round plastic lid and pried it off with his thumb and forefinger. The bottle let out a pop and the pills went onto his desk blotter.

Rios tossed one in his mouth and gulped down the water.

"Now tell me about your trip to San Thomas?" Rios sat back more comfortably.

"I was telling you. These big old Mud Men gave me the royal treatment." Rios lit a cigarette. It dangled from his lips eager to fall. His eyes lazily dragged to Carl's face.

"What did Grace Ortega say?"

Carl threw his hands up in frustration, "She didn't say anything of value to me. Just that she knew Ray Hava, she walked with him and eight others, and that she had no idea what happened. She called the Mud Men." Rios pulled opened his desk and brought out some papers. The air was stifling.

"Talk to you later." Carl backed out of the room. Rios glanced up to see him leaving. "Good-by." Carl closed the door. Rios sighed and leaned back in the chair. But the other chairs were moving. His head hurt, his mouth was still dry. Rios stared at the coffee maker. The water in the glass pitcher was staring back at him.

"God, what's happening to me. Damn it, why doesn't everything stand still?" Rios closed his eyes.

* * * * *

"Running away, running away to where?" Dan stood firmly in front of her. Dan was Doc Tapia's son: tall, good looking, and a new-found friend.

"I have to go back to Uncle Tito. I can't stay here."

Dan put his hand on Nee-nee's shoulder, "You can't go, not now. Your parents are coming, they're coming from a far away country. Please wait."

Nee-nee shook her head, eyes filled with tears, "Uncle Tito is my family. I am going to him."

Dan held her chin up and wiped the tears from her eyes, "Do you know how far away San Jaime is? At least forty miles. You can't walk that far in one day."

Nee-nee pulled away from him, "I'm not afraid of hitchhiking."

Dan shoved his hand into his blue jean pocket, "Terrific, run into Cruz and your're dead in the morning."

"I'm not afraid of Cruz. He can't hurt me."

Dan sat on the bed. "Cruz has no hold over Uncle Tito from what Gerald told you, but that doesn't mean he can't hurt you and then he will have something over Uncle Tito. If Cruz grabs you, you know there wouldn't be anything that Uncle Tito wouldn't do to get you out of trouble. You're jeopardizing Uncle Tito." Dan shook his head. "The only hope of the Pueblo, according to Gerald, is Uncle Tito. If you get him caught in Cruz's web, the whole Pueblo is lost."

Nee-nee leaned on the bedpost. Her hands were cold, her home so far away. "Gerald didn't say Cruz was looking for me."

"The worst thing you could do right now would be get near the Pueblo. Here no one knows where you live. At school the kids don't care. There is one, but never mind." Dan rubbed his nose. Nee-nee was the most beautiful girl he had ever seen.

Nee-nee sat next to him, "Who is Cruz?"

Dan shook his head, "If you don't know him, you don't want to. Just don't talk about him and stay out of his way. Stay clear of Alex, he's Cruz's kid." Nee-nee leaned over his lap putting her hand on his knee.

Then she pulled out her bedside table drawer and took out a photograph and handed it to Dan. He gasped and dropped it.

"Where did you get that?"

Nee-nee picked it off the floor, "Uncle Tito told me to keep it as evidence."

"Do you know what this means?"

"I think so, but it isn't good is it?" Their eyes, noses, lips were inches apart.

Dan took another look at the photo, "Innocent until proven guilty. I don't blame you for wanting to run off. Tomorrow I'll have the truck, I'm supposed to go into San Jaime and help Mr. Quintana with some hides and pelts Dad wants. Why don't you come with me?"

Nee-nee reached in the drawer again, pulled out a frame. "I got this to put it in so it won't get ruined by water or something, but I couldn't cut it to fit the frame."

Suddenly she glared at Dan, "First you tell me to stay away from San Jaime and now you want me to go with you. If they see me with you they'll know where I'm staying."

Dan walked over to the window, "Here comes Dad. Listen, we will tell them we're going steady. We are in a way, you know, I have been seeing a lot of you lately, huh?" Nee-nee blushed.

Doc called from the kitchen. Dan took the photo, "Better hide this in a good place." He went over to the closet and pulled out her bedroll, unrolled it, and laid the photo down inside the folds. Then he replaced it. Nee-nee pulled on her boots and they moved into the kitchen.

Nee-nee quickly put the silverware on the table and Dan disappeared outside to bring in the horses. Mrs. Tapia was washing lettuce and Doc was on the phone.

"Yeah, that'll be fine. I'll tell Dan to pick up all the hides and leather. Are you sure you want to give it all away? The bundles? Yeah, will they be as usual? Uh-huh, fine. The boy is a hard worker, he will load them up and bring them over to the office. The old ones were damaged so if you don't mind taking them back I'll have Dan run them over to you when he comes to pick up. He's fast, don't worry." Doc turned his back to the room. "As usual, keep it tight."

Mrs. Tapia smiled at Nee-nee, "Do you remember two nights ago when the Doc had that man examining himself while he was talking on the phone. Doc had that poor man unzip his pants and examine himself to find a lump in his lower abdomen?"

"Dinner was spent hoping that man was all right, because he didn't have a car." Nee-nee giggled.

"That poor soul was in a phone booth in front of Mead's Market." Mrs. Tapia let out one of her hardy truck driver laughs. "I bet Mrs. Mead got a good laugh out of it too. She thinks the whole world is crazy."

Nee-nee laughed, "Mrs. Mead talks about everyone and their strange problems. This should keep her going for days."

Mrs. Tapia gave Nee-nee a hug. "It's so much fun having you here with us, nice to have another woman in the house. There is so much to being a doctor. It is nice to have someone who doesn't talk in riddles and appreciates my food."

Doc was grilling steaks in the kitchen on the waist high brick fireplace. The long dark stained pine table was set with the white table cloth, a candelabra with five candles burning, pearl handled silverware Nee-nee had placed, cut crystal wine goblets, hand painted Mexican heavy ceramic plates, a foot long brown Papago yucca basket with a fresh loaf of French bread, and dark blue linen napkins rolled in dark wood napkin rings. The old white enamel stove, (once wood burning, now gas) held asparagus steaming in a copper double boiler and a Paul Revere aluminum pot full of freshly whipped potatoes. The family had all arrived, standing around on the kitchen brick floor, waiting for the feast, all wearing work shirts, blue jeans and boots. A tall warrior kachina stood watch on the shelf over the fireplace.

* * * * *

Rios held the phone to his ear. It was like dark licorice in his hand. "Marge, do you subsitute teach at the high school?"

"You know I do. That's where I learned the trick about moving the boys to the side of the room." Marge's voice boomed through the receiver.

"I'm looking for a young girl. She used to live with Uncle Tito and now she's disappeared."

Marge held her breath, then breathing heavily she answered, "I don't understand how the Captain of Police could not know what is going on in his backyard. Maybe it's because you don't go to the beauty parlor." Marge switched the phone to the other ear, banging it against her earring. Rios gasped at the noise.

"What do you mean, I don't know what's going on? I don't have enough hair to go to a beauty parlor."

Marge breathed into the phone again. Rios held it away from his ear. "And I'm glad of that. The girl you're speaking of is Nee-nee. She moved in with Doc Tapia last week."

Rios choked. "A week ago!" Rios' mouth was dry again. He reached for the water, missed.

"Yes, last week. Are you all right?"

"Yes, I'm fine. Got to go, see you later."

Rios tramped down the hall to Carolyn's desk. "Rios, I finally wrote up my report on the address search you sent me on. It was fascinating and scary. You were right, I should get out more. The address was way out in the boonies."

Rios took his hat off and sat down on the straight backed wooden chair in front of Carolyn's desk. "Carolyn, I called you yesterday all day long, where did you go?"

Rios leaned back in the chair, eyes closed, and he started to fall.

"Carl, help, something is wrong with the Captain." Carolyn reached over the desk and caught his jacket and held him.

Carl hobbled down the hall with his cane. He put his hands on Rios' shoulders, "Better call Marge." Carl knelt on the floor. "Captain, Captain, wake up."

He slapped Rios' face. No response. Carl put his hand on Rios' chest.

"My God, what if he's dead!" Carolyn gasped.

Carl stood up, "Carolyn, he's not dead. He's passed out cold."

Carolyn fumbled with the phone, "Marge, I think you better get down here right away. It's the Captain. I'll let you decide for yourself."

Carl's eyes met hers, "Now we better put him on the couch. We can't call Doc. Not after the information you found, Carolyn."

She ran around the desk taking hold of Rios' arms. "We'll wait for Marge to decide." They pulled Rios onto the couch.

At last they heard Marge running up the stairs.

"Where is he? I should have known something was wrong. He called me about an hour ago and didn't sound like his usual self." Marge knelt next to him. "We better call Doc."

Carl leaned over Rios straightening his jacket, "No, we can't call Doc." He almost whispered.

Marge stood up, "Well, I certainly can."

Carolyn put her arm out, "Wait, Doc is into something that we're unsure of at this time. And Rios is not someone Doc would want to treat right now."

Marge glared at them, "I am appalled at the two of you. How can you accuse Doc of anything? Just today Doc took care of Rios when his shoulder hurt so badly he couldn't sleep. Doc gave him some sleeping pills. Rios was having terrible dreams about this whole mess." Marge started towards the phone.

"Sleeping pills, what kind of sleeping pills?" Carl asked.

"I don't believe you two, my husband could be dying and you're asking questions. Dalmane, or something like that, capsules, I think."

Carl pulled Rios into a sitting position. "He has been dopey today and it could be sleeping pills."

Carolyn took the phone, "I'm going to call Mitch. He'll know what it is. If it is a heart attack, he'll be able to tell us." Her eyes waiting for Marge's reaction softened with the tone of her voice. Marge stared back at her. Carolyn dialed.

Marge pulled a straight wooden chair over to where her husband sat upright with Carl still holding onto the back of his jacket.

Carolyn made the call and sat down on the couch next to Rios. "It's a nightmare. Carl was beaten and now Rios is asleep. Oh, I didn't mean it that way." Carolyn covered her mouth with a freckled white hand.

They leaned Rios back against the couch. His face was peaceful like that of a small child waiting to be awakened.

Carolyn patted Rios on the leg. "He was trying so hard to figure it all out, but he seemed so spaced out."

Mitch burst in, his black bag hung from a short arm. He had been the only doctor in town before Doc Tapia arrived. Mitch was brought up on charges of doing too many unnecessary surgeries during his five year surgical practice in Jerez. The AMA and the Government fined him so severely he gave up his practice, sliding into an early retirement. Early for most doctors. Mitch was fifty-eight.

He opened his black bag and sat down on the other side of Rios and opened his eyelids. "Hmmmm, is he on anything?"

Marge flinched, "Yes, Doc Tapia gave him some Dalmane to help him sleep better at night." She spoke with confidence, straightening her back.

Mitch pushed Rios' head back and examined his mouth. Then he pulled out his stethoscope. There was a large bulge in Rios' jacket pocket. Mitch put his hand in and pulled out the bottle. "This what he was taking?"

Marge took the bottle. "Yes. He picked them up this afternoon." She opened the bottle and poured some into her hand. "These don't look like the same pills he gave me for my sore back."

Mitch pulled open Rios' shirt and listened to his heart. "Built like a horse." Mitch then moved the stethoscope down to his belly.

Marge stared at her husband. "Mitch, will he be all right?"

"So far hasn't hurt him. If anything he is getting a well deserved rest. Let me finish the examination. I need to check his pulse and watch his breathing."

"Marge, can I talk to you for a moment." Carolyn touched her sleeve. Marge followed Carolyn into Rios' office.

Carolyn pulled out a cigarette from a pack lying on the desk. "I've been tracking down an address your husband gave me. I went all over asking questions trying to find the street, just a road with the number on it."

Marge sat down on the edge of the desk.

Carolyn continued. "It was near San Thomas Pueblo. An old road that goes down to the river. The kids go there in the summer to drink and God knows what else. Actually it is more of a dumping ground than anything else. Well, there is the address way out there. I checked my rear view mirror out of habit and saw a green pickup truck following me. We don't know where old Cruz is, so I kept on driving."

Carolyn lit up the cigarette. "The road is way out, as I said, and it is not a place one would live. It would be too hard to drive in and out of there every day. It has a barn. Now, I couldn't get too close because I didn't want the person in the truck to know I had found what I was looking for. I drove all around and ended up on the end of a cliff road. I stopped and followed the horizon with my eyes to find my bearings. That's when I noticed the barn was directly below me."

Marge went to the door. Her back to Carolyn. "It was quiet there. Then the green truck turned around and left once I had stopped the car. There below me was Doc's truck and two other men with tall hats. I couldn't tell who they were. One walked and carried himself a lot like Cruz. Although I have only seen him once, he's a dirty character." Carolyn noticed a run in the back of Marge's stocking. She had only met Marge twice before.

Marge brushed her hair back behind her ears. "They were unloading and loading large bundles of leather hides. The strange thing was they were opening and closing each bundle, taking something small out of each one." Carolyn clicked her fingernails together, they were too long to type easily.

Marge pivoted in Carolyn's direction. Carolyn slid into Rios' chair. "They were exchanging money, that I could see."

"Marge." A voice called from the hall. Marge jumped and hurried down the hall. Rios' eyes were open.

"You best take this old man home. No more pills of any kind. These sleeping pills he's been taking are a form of morphine." Mitch buttoned up Rios' shirt.

"Morphine? But Doc said that they would just help him sleep."

Mitch stood up and stretched his short body. He picked up his black bag, "He's pretty doped up. He has a lot of this stuff in him." Mitch handed the bottle back to Marge. "This is not unusual either. Watch him, he might start seeing green men and bugs walking all over the house."

Marge grabbed at the bottle. Mitch plopped his hat on his head, "No charge." He trumped down the stairs and out the door with a bang.

"I can't believe Doc would do this. This must be the work of that pharmacist. Carl, Carolyn, you know Doc would never do this? I can't believe he would. He helps people, not this." Teeth clenched, she struck at Carl's face.

Carl reached up and stopped her arm. "Marge, whoever did this will be found out. The most important thing we can do right now is get Rios home and comfortable. God knows he's not comfortable like that." Marge's anger subsided as she walked over to the couch, shaking her head.

Rios fell over again on the couch and gave a slight moan.

Carolyn smiled, "I'll go to the school and pick up the girl. Carl, maybe between the three of us we could carry Rios down the stairs."

The front door banged open before Carl could answer. "Anybody here?" A young deep-throated voice bellowed.

A burly fellow leapt up the stairs. "Hi, is this the police headquarters?" He looked at Marge and Carl sitting on the floor and Rios passed out on the couch.

"Yes." Carl said.

The fellow smiled, "Don't tell me that's our Police Captain?" He pointed at the crumpled body on the dirty brown battered couch.

Carl put his hand on Rios' head, "Right again."

"Do you have someone who could come with me to the school? A young girl got stabbed. The nurse has sewn her up but she doesn't want to go home until the guilty party is found."

Carolyn grabbed her purse, "Sure let's go. Only we need to ask a favor of you in return?"

The fellow smiled, "Lovely lady, ask away?"

Carolyn pointed to Rios, "Would you help us carry him downstairs?"

"Me, the Police Captain, why? Is he wounded or asleep?"

Carl awkwardly arrived on his feet, "He's asleep. He has been working so hard he fell over and we can't seem to awaken him." Marge gave Carl a cutting glare.

"O.K. I can carry him. I'm a football player, strong and durable." He hoisted the Captain over his shoulder. He winked at Carolyn.

"Somebody's gotta move that foxy grey Pontiac away from the front door, or we might dent it trying to get outta here." The fellow lurched his way from one step to another. Rios' arms swung with the motion.

"Oh, yes, Carl," Marge took Carl's arm and pulled herself up. "Your car is outside."

Carl raced ahead of them. "You would never know he needed a cane, now would you?" Carolyn locked arms with Marge.

Rios was on his way home with Marge and Carl. Carolyn was being led by the big fellow back to the school. He said his name was Gerald, a friend of the girl's whose name turned out to be Nee-nee. Carolyn smiled to herself. For someone who just wanted to be a secretary all these years she was getting very involved with the active side of police work.

"It is exciting, perhaps I waited too long typing reports, now I can make my own." She brushed her short red hair back, green eyes glistened, the freckles on her nose and chin lifted with her coy grin.

* * * * *

The starched white uniform crinkled with each breath. She hovered over Nee-nee. Dedication oozed from every nurse's pore. Nee-nee tried to explain, but the starched white kept pushing her down, telling her to be still.

Finally Nee-nee fell back on the gurney. Her arm was swollen and sore. Dan should come. She knew he would come if he could.

Yesterday had been a nightmare for him, too. The truck wouldn't start. She was hidden under the tarp in the back. Doc had come out to see what was the matter. She held her breath until she almost burst. Finally they got the truck going, they were on their way.

The ride was hot and bumpy, the tarp stank of manure. When they arrived Dan went inside for what seemed forever. She heard voices around her of people she knew, some she didn't know.

At last Dan had come out and driven to the back of the Mercantile. When he parked the truck, a man had come out of the storage room and tried to lift the tarp. Nee-nee had grabbed onto the sides and held it down tightly.

Dan ran out and argued with the iron grip man. Slowly Nee-nee's fingers started to burn from grasping the tarp so tensely. She heard Dan tell the man his father was the Doc and he only wanted Dan to do the loading and unloading.

Suddenly the man swore and knocked Dan to the ground. Nee-nee was tempted to lift the tarp. Now Dan was groaning and she heard a tremendous 'wap'. But in a moment Dan whispered, ''Get out and jump in the front of the truck.'' Nee-nee moved like lightening. She glanced at the man lying on the floor of the storage room. He wore dark glasses and a fancy suit and he had a gun in his pants.

Quickly Dan unloaded the boxes his father had given him and loaded up the bundles that were lined up on the dock. Dan jumped in the cab of the truck and turned the starter but the engine clicked, started, then died. Without warning Quintana came out of the storage room yelling profoundly as he tripped over the fancy clothes man. Now everyone appeared. The ladies from the kaleidoscope factory, the butcher from the Mercantile, and the customers in the hardware department. Nee-nee squirmed under Dan's jacket lying on the floor of the truck cab.

Slowly Quintana quieted down in front of his audience. He reprimanded Dan for hurting this man, as if he didn't know who he was. Dan apologized and said it was a mistake, but the man who had now gained consciousness wouldn't listen to reason. Quintana sent everyone away and turned to Dan. Suddenly Dan stepped into the truck, closed the door, and switched on the ignition. It burst into life leaving Quintana with his mouth open and the fancy man holding his head, frantically trying to hide his gun.

* * * * *

Nee-nee tried to move her fingers with no success. As she looked up, she saw the lady come in with Gerald. She wore a tweedy green skirt, an off-white silk blouse, a policeman's blue jacket, and a matching green scarf. Orange red hair was shoulder length in back, short in front. She was smiling brightly with green eyes.

"Nee-nee, this lady is with the Police Department, she will help you. Be nice to her." Gerald saluted stiffly and walked out.

The starched white nurse came running into the room, "I'm sorry, Miss, you are not allowed in here."

Carolyn put out her hand, "I'm with the Police Department. This young lady was hurt here at school, is that right?"

The nurse pulled herself in tightening her hands, "Where is your identification?" Her lips puckered, wrinkling her white starched face.

Carolyn rummaged through her purse and found the I.D. The white nurse snatched it from her, searching out every word. 'Well, all right then, but not for long," as she marched out of the sterile room. Carolyn noticed the white silk stockings with the black straight seams.

Carolyn turned back to Nee-nee as she explained how the boy with the braids and feather whose name is Alex Cruz had run up against her in the hall at lunch time. He had pressed her to him, she tried to push him away, that's when he pulled the knife.

"At first I was frightened, then I just got mad. Who did he think he was anyway? What right did he have to do that to me? I don't know him and I certainly didn't like him. Pulling out a knife is no way to get a girl to like you. When I saw the knife, I kicked him in the . . . well . . . I kicked him. Then I shoved the knife away." Nee-nee clenched her teeth, "That's when I cut my arm."

"How does your arm feel now?"

"It doesn't feel much. The nurse put something on it." Nee- nee's eyes flashed in anger as she held up her arm. The white gauze bandage had light pink lines near her elbow.

Carolyn studied Nee-nee's profile of beauty and tenderness. Her eyes portrayed a chaos of feelings.

"Let's fix you up. Nee-nee, where would you like to go now? Would you like me to take you to Doc's?" Carolyn brushed Nee-nee's hair back with a blue brush she had pulled from her purse. She parted the long thick dark brown hair and braided it away from Nee-nee's tanned face.

"I would like to go home to Uncle Tito. I had the nurse call him." Nee-nee swung her feet over the edge of the stretcher looking for her shoes. "Are you going to arrest Alex?"

Carolyn lifted the window shade, filling the room with light. "Your uncle doesn't have a phone, does he?"

"No, the ZIA sends out someone for emergencies. They contacted Uncle Tito and called the nurse back. Are you going to get Alex Cruz?"

The chalk blue walls reflected the cold emptiness of the room on the well waxed white linoleum floors. Children's voices drifted through the open window. Dirt blew in small dust devils across the playground.

"It's a touchy subject right now, Nee-nee. We're waiting for Alex to lead us to his father. If we arrest him, well, it could throw off the trail we've worked so hard to get." Carolyn dusted off unseen lint on Nee-nee's back. Nee-nee's white blouse was worn thin enough to see the tired bra strap going across her back, her skirt had been lengthened several times. Each time the well worn hem kept its mark.

"You mean it's all right for him to go around knifing people?"

"Nee-nee, you know very well what I mean. It's complicated that's all. What he did to you was terrible and worth arresting him for, however, we're after bigger fish."

Suddenly the door to the infirmary banged shut. Uncle Tito came into the room, totally focusing on the young girl. He gave Nee-nee a gentle hug.

Seeing Carolyn, Uncle Tito backed away.

"I'm police." Carolyn extended her hand. He gave her the typical Indian hand-shake; he gently held her hand for a second then let her soft white freckled hand fall from his dark muscular fingers.

Carolyn patted Nee-nee on the back, "Call me if you need me, I'm Carolyn. The only Carolyn on the Jerez Police Force." Carolyn picked up her brown purse, threw it over her shoulder, straightened her skirt, and disappeared out the door.

Nee-nee jumped off the stretcher, "Let's go home. It is all right for me to go home now, isn't it? You'll not take me back to Doc's will you?"

Uncle Tito pushed back his stained white straw hat, "Let's go home." His braids were neatly tucked into his blue jeans.

The nurse stood in the hallway by her office. An Indian in her infirmary was not a welcome event. She did not keep them with the usual formalities of paper signing. There was much too much of that now-a-days anyway. Probably the Indian wouldn't know how to write and pointing out the inefficiency of others was not her job.

Nee-nee held back emotions as they drove down the bumpy road to her home. The old lopsided mud home stood in the same place. The dogs ran up to meet her. Home, now everything would be all right.

Uncle Tito helped her out of the truck, "Nee-nee, there are some things in the house. Don't be frightened. I had no way of knowing you would be coming home today."

Nee-nee leaned on his arm, he pushed open the door. Povi dog was lying on the rug in front of the fireplace. The dog's head and paw were bandaged. Next to her were four little pups.

"Uncle Tito, what happened to Povi dog?" Uncle Tito walked into the kitchen.

Nee-nee sat down next to her. The pups were only a few days old. As Uncle Tito fixed dinner, he didn't say a word. He just shrugged and nodded in his lack of communication, and Nee-nee was too tired to press him for answers. When Uncle Tito was ready to talk he would. After dinner Nee-nee pulled her old quilt up around her in bed. It smelled of dried pinon and old perfume. Her arm throbbed a dull pain that lashed out at her whenever she bent it.

Later in the night the fire crackling in the fireplace awoke her. Uncle Tito was gone, so was the truck. She gently pulled on the door and a pale moon peered back at her. The crickets chirped in the stillness of the black night. Nee-nee searched for a star. Venus poked through a high thin cloud.

"I wish I may I wish I might have the wish I wish tonight." Nee-nee opened her eyes wide. "Oh, please God, stop the killings in the world. Let things be as they are to grow peacefully and in harmony like Uncle Tito says. Don't let things change too fast."

Nee-nee leaned on the door frame. If only they had a phone, she could call Debbie. Poor Debbie, her life had become complicated, too. Gerald had spent the last date with her talking about Doc's oldest daughter. He spoke of her in colorful compliments. Nee-nee smiled, Doc's daughter was twenty-two and gorgeous.

Tuesday, Day 5

Rios opened his eyes, the room walked away from him. He blinked and the room walked back on long legs. Rios tried to speak. All that came out were purple light bulbs.

His mind searched for an answer. The medication. He vaguely remembered someone saying something about capsules.

Marge eased into the room, "Dominique, are you there?" Rios opened his eyes, Marge was smaller than he remembered. He reached out to her, her hand to him, her hand grew and grew. He rolled away from it and felt sick to his stomach.

"Dominique, would you like something to eat?" Marge pulled the covers over his back. He was wet with sweat.

"Dominique, Carolyn is here to fill you in on what is happening. There are a lot of skeletons in closets."

Rios closed his eyes. Skeletons in closets did not happen. Cruz was cardboard. Cruz was a phony and of thinly cut cardboard. If Cruz was caught, a new piece of cardboard would appear, it would have to be Alex Cruz. Cardboard people trying to become real. They had to kill the real people to get ahead. Cardboard people have no feeling. They act out of their corrugated shells.

Marge tiptoed into the living room and sat on the edge of the easy chair. She offered Carolyn another sugar cookie from the Mexican blue enamel plate.

Carolyn watched Marge, "He will be better soon, just wait and see, soon." Carolyn gave her a reassuring smile.

"We found Cruz. He was in the back of Martinez' Tractor and Trailer Store on Second Street. He had been hiding there for some time. He was meeting his son outside the back alley for cigarettes and a change of clothes now and then. Alex never suspected he was being followed. He drove to the dump of a house that he lives in and picked up some papers for Cruz, then drove to the alley. The Greek, Catrados, our chief deputy, grabbed him."

Carolyn set her cup on the saucer and reached over and picked up Moses. Moses purred. "They didn't catch Alex. He's a slippery fella, slippery like his father. Poor Nee-nee was upset when we couldn't arrest Alex. That shiftless skunk is on the loose again."

Marge yawned, "Excuse me. Why didn't the deputies surround the alley and get them both?"

Carolyn winced, "Well, we have a volunteer deputy system. They did the best they could under the circumstances. The alley opens to six or seven shops including the beauty parlor that has an underground connecting air vent with the two buildings on either side. It was tough. They did a good job to get Cruz."

"Where's Nee-nee now? Did she go back to Doc's?"

"The girl is with Uncle Tito and we're expecting something big to happen in the Pueblo soon. The ZIA Police are scared without Cruz. We have called the FBI, but the ZIA Police won't let them on the reservation. Evidently they need to be called in by the ZIA or invited in."

Marge poured more tea in the pale almond china cups. "What is Nee-nee doing back in the Pueblo? Isn't that dangerous?"

"Well, I don't know. I think it's better that she's with people she loves. Doc's son Dan is very fond of Nee-nee and he said he'd drive over sometime today. The two of them are very good looking, but Nee-nee has a name that simply doesn't fit her. Maybe her mother was Indian and her father an Irishman." Carolyn laughed.

"At the beauty parlor they have been saying that her parents were called and are expected to arrive anytime," Marge said.

"Poor girl, she has had enough moving around for awhile. Let me tell you about Carl's expedition to the Pueblo yesterday. Carl has never met Mr. Quintana so he got this brain storm. He borrowed your husband's costume kit and put on a moustachio, long side burns, and carried a long cigarette holder. Actually, he looked more like a comedian trying out for the part of Cyrano. He took the name Dr. Fuedalstein, an anthropologist from Stanford. He went to the Mercantile and studied their rugs. As he was leaving he sat down and pretended he was having trouble breathing. Mr. Quintana immediately came to his rescue."

Marge smiled, "Carl looks bad already, he hardly had to pretend."

Rios moaned from the bedroom. "Marge, can I have some water? My tongue is sore."

"I can't seem to get used to him being here in the day. Every time he calls out, it scares me to death. Sure, Dom, I'm coming." She went into the bedroom — and returned.

"All right, go on. He's already asleep. I bring him the water and he's out, sound asleep. What did Mr. Quintana do then?" Marge sat on the couch.

Carolyn lit a cigarette, blowing the smoke away from Marge. "Quintana took Carl in the back office. He had piles of cartons stacked all over. He offered Carl all kinds of medication. Carl couldn't remember the name of the medication that he was supposed to take so conveniently, of course, Quintana came out with more than enough. Carl noticed white powder on the floor around one of the cartons. He made a point to step in it on the way out. Later it checked out to be cocaine."

Marge put her tea cup on her lap. "Dangerous powder to leave lying on the floor. Did Carl arrest him?"

"No, we decided, or rather Carl decided to bring them in today for questioning. So we shall see."

Marge sighed, "Things are rotten in Denmark. What about the Halfway

House, does he supply them with drugs?"

"No, Doc brings the necessary dope with him when he comes to examine the patients."

Marge's eyes widened. "So the two of them may be in this together?"

Carolyn stood up. "I better get back. You tell that old man of yours to straighten up and fly right. Enough spacing out, time to get back to work."

* * * * *

Carl showed Mr. and Mrs. Quintana into Rios' office. His was the only official office in the building. Carl brought two large grey mug books. He lay them open on the table beside Mr. Quintana. A cork board above the table was covered with Wanted posters. Mr. Quintana sat down on the wooden high backed chair to review the books.

Mrs. Quintana fumbled with her purse, glanced at the floor, then sat in the chair that Carl pushed towards her. Her flowered pink and purple wrap-around skirt fell to her calves. She had a fluffy white fiesta blouse on with a bumble bee pin on her wide lace collar. Her eyes shown of soft amber, outlined with a dark brown eyeliner. Her cheeks, flushed white, clearly showed the pink blush. Her unmade lips were tight.

Carl guessed her age at about thirty-five. Mrs. Quintana's fingers kept playing nervous games with her car keys which had been drawn from her purse.

Mr. Quintana appeared calm. His white short sleeved ivy league shirt was open at the collar and he smiled, not showing his teeth.

"It's very interesting how many drugs go through the Pueblo in one week, don't you think?" Carl pushed his thick glasses back on his nose.

"Mr. Quintana, do you have any employees on drugs?"

"What do you mean by that? Are we supposed to find murderers or drug dealers?" Tension was building as Quintana flipped page after page.

Carl packed his pipe, "Both."

Quintana pushed back the book, "All right, you want to get down to it, then let's get down to it."

Mrs. Quintana dropped the car keys. She grabbed them up in her shaking white hand nervously watching her husband, fear in her eyes.

Carl stood up and lit his pipe, "Quintana, you are dealing in drugs, are you not?"

Mrs. Quintana gave a whimper.

"Hush, Mary. Carl, that's a heavy accusation, isn't it?" Quintana turned to the pictures before him. The faces were all turned to one side.

Carl smiled, "You and Doc, huh, trying to survive?" Quintana stood up. Carl let the pipe smoke rise to his face.

"See here, I don't know anything about Doc, but yes, we got into some dirty dealings. But we're out of it. May we leave now?" He lifted Mary's arm but she didn't move. Either her legs would not hold her, or she had no desire to leave.

Carl pulled the pipe from his teeth, "Hava knew, didn't he?" Carl leaned his leg against the desk.

Mr. Quintana frowned, "Hava knew too much about a lot of things. He had a way about him. People took him into their confidence. Hava never would have hurt that confidence either. I don't know about Hava. I didn't kill him, God knows, I loved him like a brother."

Mrs. Quintana burst into tears. Carl paced the room, filling it with smoke as he spoke, "What do you want out of?"

Quintana retorted, "I want out of this place, out of the police station."

Mrs. Quintana turned on her husband, "You, you, you, you, everything is what you want. You wanted us to be rich. Just for a while that's what you said. If my poor father could see me now he would be proud. I've had it with standing by you. I held up believing that it was really to our benefit. But now, with people dead . . . Hava gone, he was a real person, not a liar like you."

She stood shaking with anger, pointing her nail-polished finger at her husband, "You, you, all you can think of is you. The children have not been given a chance to live, because all you can think of is your needs and your wants and we have to circle around those. You got into the leather and hide business knowing so well it was a front for dope. You tried to tell me it was so right, that you could get out of it, then you almost kill Dan Tapia, and you threaten Nee-nee, and throw Uncle Tito out of the store."

Quintana leapt at her but she moved quickly to Carl's side, her hand on Carl's arm as she continued to point at her husband. "You should be locked up. Then we would be free to enjoy our lives instead of feeling we are paying penance for your evil ways that you so easily justify."

Carl guided her out into the hall.

"Carolyn, could you help me with Mrs. Quintana?" Carolyn rose to the rescue.

Back in the office Quintana was white, his upper lip was quivering, his hands shaking, "That woman has never spoken so many words in her whole life." He sat down hard on the edge of the mug book table.

"What she said isn't true, not a word of it. You can't go on the words of a crazy woman. I knew some day she would finally crack. It's in her family." Quintana walked to the window. "There isn't one word of truth in what she said. I have spent my entire life, a fortune as a matter of fact, looking after that woman. She has taken all kinds of medication. She gets these terrible cramps every month and they drive her to exhaustion. She won't touch me. If, oh, yes, if I give her some special medicine she's all right. You must forgive her. You can even call the insurance agency. Do you know how much it costs me to insure that woman? A fortune. Then she intimidates me like that in front of you. Poor woman, she's to be pitied." He shook his head and turned to Carl.

Meanwhile, Carl took out the costume box and slipped on the mustachio he had worn the day before.

"Oh; not you. There was something about those eyes, now I know." Carl took the mustache off and let it drop on the desk. Quintana let out a sigh.

"You think we could work out a deal? I can be flexible when I have to be. Something said in the right place . . ."

Carl lit his pipe, turned on the desk light, and put some of Rios' coffee on to brew. Rios would surely approve.

"It's time for names and dates." Dark clouds had covered the sky and wind blew through the building. Quintana buried his head in his hands. It was going to be a long afternoon.

In the other room Carolyn handed Mary Quintana some coffee. "Mary, what you did was to hold onto life. You had to do something."

"He will hate me now. We tried to do what would make him happy. He has a hard time dealing with people. It is so much easier for him, when he can be the all-giving, understanding, and the loving rich man. It was awful before we came here. He yelled at the boys, and tried to attack a maid we had for years. Soon, I hope it will all be over and we can rest." Mary's face wrenched in pain.

*****

Marge pulled a blanket over her knees. The bathroom light cast a dull glow on the bedroom floor. Rios was still asleep, off and on for almost two days. Mitch told her to just let him sleep it off.

Marge picked up the newspaper. The political campaign dinner had been successful, the Governor had made his money-making speech, and the restaurant had made a bundle. The rain changed to sleet outside. Marge yawned and stretched, pushing the recliner all the way back she closed her eyes and drifted into sleep.

Dominique Rios' mind began the replay of a long forgotten time . . .
Grandma was walking me to school, reminding me for the millionth time I was adopted for "No grandson of mine would drag his feet like you." *She stopped. We were standing in front of Mr. Grant's white picket fence.*

"You see them roses, son?"

That's all I could see in his little lot. He had the smallest lot on the block. The path (if there ever had been one) from the white gate to the narrow brown porch with the door was nothing but bathtub after bathtub of dirt filled with roses, all different colors, heights, smells.

"I was married once to a man who loved and raised roses. He spent all his time at work in town or in the rose garden. My life with him was a trial. One trial after another."

She shook her head. Fluffy white bangs bounced back over her grey bun pinned tightly on the back of her head.

"Life was climbing a rose. Thorn after thorn, being pricked, hurt, and ignored until you came to a beautiful rose flower. Then life was sweet and beautiful. The rose flower would fade, petals would fall and quickly you grab the branch." She jerked my arm up over my head until it hurt.

"Thorns, one thorn after another you pull yourself up. Maybe you come to a flower bud. It opens and life is sweet, or a high wind comes up and it's blown away from you and you're back to thorns." Her strong grey eyes fixed on Mr. Grant's roses with severe hate.

"My husband died in northern Pennsylvania. Now the tops of all his rose bushes are thorns. When I moved here to help your Ma, the roses had grown into a forest of thorns. I'm glad your Ma, adopted Ma that is, married a mechanic. You're late boy, don't dawdle." She shoved my shoulder, my purple plaid shirt fell forward wrinkled on my chest.

When we got to the Catholic Church, Grandma pulled me to the other side of the street. It wasn't until later that I found out why. Grandma was a God-fearing woman. She didn't approve of drink or gambling. That Catholic church did both every Tuesday and Thursday night. So I walked around it to and from school.

Rios rolled on his left side. His shoulder screamed in pain as he remembered.

Ma was pregnant when I was eight. It was winter in Pennsylvania and cold clear through. Ma would get up at night to use the bathroom, the thin floor boards squeaked.

That was when everything started going bad. One evening at dinner some man came pounding on the door. Dad answered it. A rich man with a cigar had a fancy car that broke down. The man was wet with snow and full of money. He kept pulling out green dollars and laying them on the table.

Ma watched. Her thin white face made her emerald blue eyes sharp and defined. Her lips were set in the usual puckered, but closed position.

Dad kicked my foot under the table. "Let's go."

We went out into the snow. I steered, he pushed, and we got the car into the garage. Dad shut the big garage doors. But the wood stove wouldn't light. Dad was cussing. He threw down the bellows and started in on the big car. It was the biggest car I ever remember seeing.

Dad started the engine. Turned it off, worked, turned it on, cussed, never stopping. Finally he yelled at me to turn the engine. I sat in the plush grey seat, then slid down and hit the gas pedal turning on the ignition. All I could smell was stale cigars.

It was clouding up in the garage and breathing was hard. I could hear my Dad's cough. He had it when I came eight years ago. Dad banged and swore. Then he started to cough again.

My eyes were rolling around in my head. I ached all over. I jumped out and felt the air pushing me down. I couldn't see Dad so I ran upstairs, screaming, yelling, scared.

Grandma grabbed me, lifting my feet off the ground. "Stop that yelling, You're gonna frighten that baby into comin' too soon."

I screamed what had happened. Grandma dropped me on the floor.

Next thing I knew I was in bed. People were talking ouside my curtain that separated me off from the kitchen. Someone asked about Dad.

"He's alive, but for how long it's up to God." Someone brushed my curtain. I shrank under the quilts.

Grandma said, "Let the boy be. If he dies it's God's blessing. Soon we'll have our own blood relative to carry on the family name."

The footsteps faded away. Ma came later with some soup. She was skin and bones and blue emerald eyes, except for the large round protrusion from her belly.

There were tears in her eyes. She put the soup on the floor and sat on my quilted mattress.

"I love you Dominique. You have been given a strong name. You are good and kind. You will make us proud, I know it." She spoon fed me the soup.

The light in the house was always yellow grey and Dad needed a humidifier, and boiling water. The windows were covered with yellow cheese cloth to keep out direct sun. Dad coughed all the time. Bloody stained sheets hung across the kitchen. Grandma had said let him die, he can't breathe.

To earn a living Ma worked hard baking bread. I delivered it. Grandma changed sheets, Dad coughed. Ma slept with me at first. Then I slept on a blanket in the kitchen on the floor by the stove.

The baby came, a girl. Grandma was disappointed, she wanted a boy. Then the baby went, we had a funeral. Ma cried all the time. She would hug me and stare into my eyes with tears running down her sad thin white face.

Ma died and that was the beginning of freedom. I was sad to see Ma covered with dirt in the spring with flowers starting to bloom.

Grandma and I stood there apart. Her eyes fixed on the grave next to Ma's, the little girl that was her blood line. I was watching the men's faces as they threw the dirt.

Dad was still coughing. Grandma fixed herself some tea after the funeral. Then she packed and was gone.

Now I took care of Dad. I stole bicycles, changed and repaired them and when I had enough I opened a bike store in the garage. Lots of people were suspicious, but it worked long enough to get us two tickets to Alcala.

The people said a dry warm climate would make Dad well. So I dressed him, and leaned him on my nine year old body and put us on a train. We didn't have any extra money for food, but we made it.

Dad got better. He wired Pennsylvania for what was left of his money and we lived in a lean-to by the railroad track. I went to public school at my convenience.

I stole, got caught, was verbally reprimanded, and went to school for a month then started all over.

Dad fixed things, coughed, drank, and sang songs. We had a great time. Dad's eyes sparkled when he drank and I never had to take a bath if I didn't want to.

Rios rolled over in the bed. The sheets were wet. He opened his eyes but the light was still too bright.

Dad died quietly one night. I got up, lit a match, then a cigarette and stared at his face. It took two days to find someone who would help me bury him. That's one of the drawbacks of being a loner, finding people who will help you or even believe you.

They buried him in the town's Potter's Field. They dug a hole and put his body wrapped in blankets into it. Dad's burial was more real, I could see his body, the shape and frozen position. Ma was buried in a box in the ground, more impersonal.

Women came to the lean-to. They grabbed me, hustled me, and tried to catch me. They didn't though, I always got away.

Grandma came in a big car, with a big old fat man, and diamonds on her fingers. She patted my head, and carted me off to a boy's home.

Prison is bad, but it's worse when you're thirteen. I was beaten raw, picked on by peers, pushed, prodded, poked for three years. Never saw a woman the whole time I was there and was beginning to doubt their existence. But I graduated with good grades into the world . . .

Rios rubbed his eyes. They no longer burned. The cat purred, pushing his way to Rios's chin. It was dark.

"Marge? Marge, it's over Marge where are you?" Rios' voice came out a cracked whisper.

The air was heavy in the bedroom. Rios read the clock, eleven-thirty. He slid his feet over the side of the bed, pushed on his slippers, grabbed his robe and tiptoed through the house to the living room, startling Marge who was alseep on the couch.

She jumped up, hugging his sweat-damp body.

"Would you like something to drink?"

"Do we have decaffeinated tea?" Rios fell back on the couch.

Marge went into the kitchen and came back with the tea and some aspirin.

Rios took the cup, "Is this the aspirin that won't give you a stomach ache?"

Marge smiled, "Is there an aspirin that gives you a stomach ache?"

Rios shook his head 'no'. Moses crept along the floor hiding behind Marge's feet.

"Who's the guard dog?" Rios pointed to Moses. Marge laughed, "He's great to have around. I told you he guards me when you're gone for the night. Now do you believe me?"

"What a lady, she has two men to guard her."

"You had me worried."

Rios tried to stand. She held his arm and he leaned on her shoulder to the bedroom.

"Any news on the bad guys?"

"You'll have to wait until morning."

Rios pulled her down next to him, "Good. I'm busy tonight anyway."

Marge nudged out of his grip, "I want you alive in the morning."

Wednesday: Day 6

Rios pushed the coffee pot against the books on the shelf. "Carl, the only thing to do is bring Doc in and question him. With luck he'll tell us what he knows. Get to it."

Carl nodded, picked up his cane, limping out of the room. "Sir, don't you think you should sit down?"

"Carl, did you fingerprint your car? By the way, I'm glad to see you got it back?"

"I fingerprinted it after we dropped you off. The only print I could raise was mine. The inside had been wiped clean. There were traces of tar on the floor by the gas pedal. I sent it in with Jose yesterday, they called this morning. It is a kind of tar they use only in Arizona to flat-top areas of the road that buckle after a heavy snow."

"Arizona, who do we know that has been to Arizona? Cruz is not alone. Somehow I knew it. He's not all that efficient on his own." Rios waved as Carl disappeared through the door.

Carl knocked on Carolyn's desk as he went by. 'You're mumbling again?" Carolyn took off her earphones, "What a face you just made. Can I hear the words that went with it?"

"I heard you mumbling again, with no one around to appreciate the comment."

"Mrs. Quintana said her husband was irresistibly irritating. What do you think of that?"

Carl laughed, "I'm glad I'm not him."

"Poor lady, she was very upset. Her husband going into the dope business. That's a real creep. If I married I certainly would want to know if my chances of staying out of jail were good, fair, or lousy."

Carolyn shuffled the typewritten papers on her desk. "Do you think Rios is all right? I mean he's not read a report since he came back. Did anyone tell him Cruz was in J-A-I-L?" Carolyn squinted.

"Well, to be perfectly honest, yes. I told him about Cruz, and I told him about the reports I had read. But the biggie is, will he hold up. And if I may ask, Miss Carolyn, who do you suspect of murdering half-starved persons?" Carl held the pipe clenched in his teeth.

"Well, since you put it that way, I'm not sure of the outcome of my statement. However, if an outcome is necessary, and you feel my opinion is valuable, then I shall proceed to give it to the honorable askee." She thumped her pencil on the desk.

"Askee? So, I am being accused of being the askee, is it?" Carl frowned.

"Well, no actually. I you are doing the asking then you are the asker, I would be the askee. Right?" Carolyn smiled.

"Since you put it that way, I would rather be the asker. Please go on, I'm convinced the main staple of the puzzle piece lies in your answer."

"Lies, or lays in it?"

"Well, what do you wish to do with it? If you want it to go somewhere then perhaps we should have it lay, then arise and go forth. If it's lie, then there it lies forever." Carl gave a wink.

"Sir, if this conversation is to go further, then I must request that we stick to the subject. My opinion has been requested and being of the female sex and one who is discussing a fatal incident, I feel you should hear me out."

"Please, I await you."

"I suspect the following people. First the loyal and faithful wife. Second, the loyal and faithful wife, third, the lover or mistress. There, now ask me why?"

Carl stood up, pushed his glasses up on his forehead, "For heaven's sake, why?"

"I think it's poisoning and so do you, and as everyone knows, poisoning is a woman's trick. For centuries people have been poisoning people and thoroughly enjoying it. Lost souls with thoughtless husbands, and long lost lovers returning from long journeys to find women married to rich, fat, and dirty ol' men."

Carl shook his head, "Ruthless women, I would rather not be involved with that type. Give me a basic honest hard working rock and roller type any day. Too intellectual a woman leads to premeditation and terminal disorders of the mind."

Rios grumbled coming in from his office. "Very well put. Have either of you stumbled across photography equipment, besides your run in with Cruz, Carl?"

"No. Is there something fishy in the darkroom?"

Rios dropped his unlit cigarette into Carolyn's ashtray. "There may be murder with the darkroom chemicals. Hava wasn't into photography, was he?"

Carolyn pushed Rios' cigarette back on the ashtray, "What would photography have to do with this?"

Rios cocked his head, "I remember a photography course I once took, the chemicals could be fatal and all were warned to stay away from inhaling or touching the stuff."

Carl pondered, "So . . . while the man is working he somehow gets a whiff of this stuff and bang." He slapped his hands together. "Although he was in his pajamas flat on his back in bed."

"Let's be on the look out for photography equipment and check out Cruz's place after we finish with Doc. What's say?"

"We're with you." Carl pointed to Carolyn. "Old long eye over here, she's sure not to miss a trick."

Rios picked up his cigarette, "Long eye?" Carl touched Carolyn's nose, "It's here on the end of her nose. She's a sharp lady. What do you think of Mrs. Hava being suspect numero uno?"

Rios lifted his shoulders, "If she's guilty we need proof without a doubt. She is a favorite of the Pueblo. Also, she's the cousin of the ZIA Chief and sister to this year's Governor of the Pueblo. She may very well be suspect numero uno, but she has all the right connections to put her out of reach. We'll see."

Carl pulled on his jacket. Rain was coming down in torrents outside. "I'm not envious of me today. I have to go and arrest the Doc."

Carolyn glared at the two of them, "How can you do that?" Carl answered, "Just for interrogation. See you soon." Carl flung his English cabbyhat on his high forehead. The front door banged.

The phone rang, Carolyn answered. Rios sat down noticing her surprised expression.

"Boss, there's been another body found, possible homicide, at the Mervinstride Hotel. A drunk, two hour's ago, body just found by the owner cleaning up. They asked for you."

Rios straightened his back and buttoned his denim jacket. "Call me when Carl's back with Doc."

The Mervinstride Hotel was dark inside with only one small light bulb hanging over the Bus Depot's worn yellow-brown desk. Rios stamped his boots, knocking mud on the worn yellow-green carpet.

"Hello, anyone here?" A small lady with a lopsided grin hobbled out of a room, dragging her bedroom slippers.

"Captain Rios, the body is in here." She jerked her head to the side letting fuzzy brown hair reveal a bald spot on the back of her head. Rios remembered Carl's report on this woman claiming rape last week. The guilty party turned out to be her girlfriend.

A large woman with short cut hair, dressed in men's clothing met them at the door. Five or six people from other rooms followed the Captain down the dark corridor. A willowy unshaven man appeared at the end of the corridor. He weaved down the long hall and fell against the deeply stained lime green wall. Rios pushed ahead of the small woman, stepping into a dark faded room the size of a large walk-in closet. There was no bathroom.

The stench was strong. The only window was broken, air blowing into the dismal space. A man lay across the bed with his mouth and one glazed brown eye open, a bottle of whiskey in his hand.

"How long has he been here?" Rios leaned over the man's head.

"He's not supposed to be here. He broke in through the window, and crashed on the bed. Stupid jerk, I never would let him stay here. This here's a reputable place. We don't let just anybody come in here." The woman dressed in men's clothing approached Rios. She had a butch hair cut, tobacco stains on

74

her front teeth, a hairline mustache shaded her upper lip.

"He's a drunk who is always causing trouble. We don't like the likes of his kind." She shoved up her sleeve, exposing a tattoo of a nude woman.

Rios touched the glass on the window, it had been broken a long time. Outside were bent beer cans and used toilet paper. Rios tried to remove the bottle from the drunk's hand, it wouldn't budge.

"I can get it for you." The woman grabbed the bottle, reaching around Rios, knocking him forward.

"Just leave it." Rios smelled the man's mouth. Booze, a lot of booze all around. Rios stood up, holding his head. Rios closed his eyes for a moment. The smell was terrible.

"What's that smell?"

The small lady walked over to the gas stove in the corner. "It's da stove, da gas leaks all da time. Dat's why me and her kept da room locked for we didn't want nobody comin' in here and gettin' kilt." She quickly glanced at the tall woman for approval.

Rios shook his head, "Good thinking except someone did come in here and now they're dead. Does the Health Department know you have a faulty stove?"

The woman grunted loudly. "No, we was going to fix it when there was the money to be had to do it." Rios walked out into the hall.

"Keep this room locked, We'll send the Medical Examiner around to check things out. Also, I will have to inform the Health Department and this fellow's next of kin." Rios walked down the hall to get away from the fumes. "Do you know his name?"

The small woman led him to the Bus Depot desk. Her head just barely appeared over the top. She boosted herself up on a stool. Her brown hair hung raggedly to her shoulders. One brown eyebrow went full length across both eyes.

"Yes, his name is Juan Vaquero. He is from San Jaime. He comes here and wants to sell everybody doper, bad doper dat he peek up in the Pueblo. We don't do doper here, so we send him away. I tell you dis here where no one else can here. I have problems with my girlfriend; she like to do doper sometimes and den get it on. So we don't like to have doper around. You know?" Small black hairs on her chin moved as she spoke.

Rios broke his stare from her mouth. It spoke without moving. Rios took out his notebook.

"Where did he live in San Jaime?" The small woman tilted her head. "I don't know dem things. I don't go to his house or nothing." She pulled the worn torn pink house coat tighter around her body and shoved her hands into stretched pockets.

Rios leaned against the desk, "Does he have any family here in town or in San Jaime?"

She scratched her thin ragged brown bangs, "No, I don't know dem things eider. You kinda cute. You live wayout with your missus, huh?" She pulled on the pockets.

Rios leaned back against the door, pushing his hat back, "Miss, did he come in today and ask for a room?"

"What do you take me for, of course not. He stays for free at da Halfway House in San Jaime. His sister put im dere, she say dat her business is at da beauty parlor, it's over dere, and she no need any doper drunk coming around and pushing her customers to buy his bad doper. I don't want to tell you no more, if you don't like me den I don't like you. You ready to leave or what?"

Rios put his pencil in his pocket. "No. I want to talk to the boarders who have rooms next to Juan's. Do you have a room where I could talk to them privately?"

"Sure, I do, you can use our room." She pulled her housecoat up and march-ed down the hall.

Rios' headache plunged harder into his head as he followed her into a large bedroom. She turned on the light, another bare bulb hanging from the center of the room. The once white walls were laden with graffitti. The rug was worn from daily traffic to the kitchen, bathroom, front door.

Rios glanced at the naked bulb. His pupils slipped back into the center of his head and then reappeared. He sat down on the chair. It held his weight, remind-ing him of the weight it had held up in the past by the grease and residue that still clung to it.

"Would you ask one of the boarders to come in?" The little woman curtsied, "Sure ting, boss." She slammed the door behind. Rios put his hands to his head. It was still there. Maybe Marge was right, he should have stayed in bed for another week.

"Here is one of de next door guys." She pushed in a timid woman with tired breasts hanging under her housecoat. The housecoat must be the Mervinstride uniform, he thought. The woman was ageless. She was worn, her femininity tarnished.

Rios put his hand out to the bed. She shuffled over and sat down. Rios raised his pencil and cleared his throat.

"Did you hear anything strange last night?"

The woman smiled, "Last night was Carlos' turn. He makes a lot of the noise in bed, I didn't hear anything but the man."

"What man was that?" She leaned her head back, "Carlos, I told you, he was noisy. He is always noisy, man."

Rios wrote down, suspect on left side did not hear any sounds of trouble. The woman stared at Rios. "You want to make whoopie here?"

Rios closed his note pad, "Have you ever seen Juan Vaquero before?"

"Sure, I know him. He's a big friend of Red's, she comes on Tuesdays and Thursdays. They get it on big."

Rios' eyes widened. Red was big, she would do things in a big way. He kept from smiling.

"I have to go to the bathroom, can I go now?"

"Yes, you can go." She waddled out of the room.

Perhaps he had seen enough. "You ready for one more?" The little woman pushed in a tall man dressed in a fine black suit, but it was wrinkled from the cuff of his pants to the collar around his neck. As the man moved to the light, stains appeared as if by magic. The man had on a tie, worn boots, and his hair was combed neatly in place with a month's build up of grease.

"Please have a seat?" Rios stood, offering him the chair.

"No thank you, I would rather stand." Rios put his hand out to introduce himself with a handshake. Then he saw that the man's hands were shaking.

"I didn't do anything." The man had firm conviction written all over him. His Spanish nose gave him a profile of pride and honor from the old country.

"Did you hear any strange noises last night? Anything you might think suspicious?" Rios put his pencil to the notebook pad.

"No, I never hear strange noises. Especially at night. It's not healthy." The man started to shake his head.

Rios pushed the heavy chair over to the man, "Please, sit down."

The man sat abruptly. "He was my friend, he brought me dope. Now he's gone. Where will I get it from?" Tears ran down the man's cheeks. Rios wiped his forehead.

"Juan brought you drugs?" Rios dared to sit on the bed.

"Not just drugs, he would laugh a lot. He loved Red and he wanted to marry her. He sold us the bad doper that the Halfway House threw out. He really wanted to get out of this town. He was real worried lately. San Jaime is full of snakes."

"Do you know Cruz?"

"Everybody knows Cruz. He and his son, they have dealt in doper, too." The man's eyes lit up, then a frown.

"Do you know Red?"

The man flinched, "She was my girl until he came along. But it was okay, I got a lot of free doper. This ain't such a bad life onced you get used to it. We was all in the army together. Well, not all of us, but a lot. That's where we got on the doper."

Rios' head started to pound. He took his hat off, there wasn't any place clean enough to put it so he put it back on his head.

Rios walked back to the station. As he entered, Carolyn was licking envelopes. "Please call Mitch, ask him to look into the Mervinstride Hotel. Also, call the Health Department. Tell them to bring out the fumigator, that place is terrible. The hotel could kill you just standing in it. What a filth bed. Did Carl return with Doc?" He shook the rain from his hat.

"Yes, he did. They're in your office. Couldn't you shake that hat outside before you come in. You're getting water all over the desk. Listen to the thunder." The phone rang, Carolyn picked it up.

Rios took a deep breath. This was going to be very difficult. He'd been friends with Doc a long time. Rios stomped his boots all the way down the hall to the door. He pushed it open and was met with a room full of pipe smoke.

Rios hung up his hat and went to the coffee maker. He poured the old coffee into the stainless steel sink, rinsed out the pyrex pitcher and filled it with water. He poured freshly ground coffee into the top of the machine and placed the water in the top. It hissed, sputted, then quieted down to a soft purr.

Carl knocked the pipe tobacco out of his pipe. Doc coughed. Rios pushed the window open. "Carl, would you call Red and ask her if she could come up later."

Fresh wet air billowed into the room. Doc sat in the straight wooden chair. His eyes red, his nose running, his hands nervous.

"Rios, I want to make one thing perfectly clear. All I gave you was a prescription. What the pharmacist put in there, well, should be what I prescribed."

Rios sat back in his chair and put his feet up on the corner of his worn wooden desk. Rios watched the coffee maker. Steam was rising over the pyrex container. Weather was sleeting into the room. Rios leaned back further and closed the window, brushed off his pants, lit up a cigarette. He put it out.

"You called in the prescription before I ever got there. The pharmacist was waiting for me when I arrived." Rios leaned over to the shelf. He took two mugs off the miniature wooden tree. "Black or cream and sugar?"

"Black, your coffee is too good to wreck. Rios, I did not drug you. I just want you to know that?" Doc ended it with a question. Rios handed him the mug.

"Doc, we checked with the pharmacy first thing. They have a copy of the prescription you called in and it matched the prescription you handed me. It was on file." Rios sipped at his coffee. He put his feet back up.

"Doc, the problem is too much lying going on around here. Someone is found out and then they deny it to protect someone else. Who are you protecting?"

Doc took his pocket watch out of his vest pocket, "I have surgery in thirty minutes."

Rios leaned forward, dropping his feet to the floor. "You are not going anywhere until this is cleared up. There are too many bodies, very dead bodies, without any explanation. So, let me ask you this directly. Are you dealing in dope?"

"By dope, I suppose you are referring to drugs?"

"Yes, drugs. Lethal drugs, that are almost impossible to trace."

"You want a straight answer?"

"Yes."

"I do not deal in fatal drugs. Although any drug is fatal if not used correctly."

"I'm talking about psychedelic drugs?"

"You mean causing delusions, or visions, the kind of thing that wrecks the mind?"

"You got it."

"Rios, there isn't a drug on the market today that doesn't have some side affect. It would be impossible for me to say I don't prescribe that kind of drug. However, I do not prescribe that kind of drug just so the patient can have visions."

"You only cure the ill, is that right?"

"Yes. To prevent illness or to cure one. That would be the only way I would prescribe a drug of any kind."

"So, if you were to meet someone out in the prairie and give them medication, it would be just to heal the sick?"

"Yes. Why out in the prairie?"

"Perhaps . . . down by the river would be a better analogy?"

"Down by the river, out in the prairie, Rios, you're talking in riddles."

"There's a commune out near Alacante, isn't there?"

"How in the hell should I know?" Doc straightened in his chair.

"Because you went out there with the ZIA doctor and saved his life. The hippies out there shot him. Isn't that right?"

"I suppose so."

"Are you giving them drugs now to prevent and cure disease or are you giving them drugs for visual reasons?"

"Someone has to. Someone has to help them."

"Do you take money for the medication you give them?"

"No, of course not. I would not do that. They need the medication and I give it to them."

"So the drugs were medication?"

"Most definitely."

"How do you know what to give to whom, if they came down in trucks, they couldn't possibly have brought everyone with them. How did you give each one the proper dose?"

"It is written on slips of paper, the age, the weight, the diet and the symptoms of each individual up there. There were two nurses living up there. Beautiful young girls, trying to help out, trying to used the education they ran away from to help the people they love. It's all above board and professional. Here's a paper with someone's name.

Doc produced a narrow green paper. It had a name written on it, next to the age. Ten years old, fever, swollen glands, only fifty pounds.

"You have been doing this weekly for two months now, is that right?"

"That is correct."

"You are still protecting someone, who?" Rios reached over and poured himself more coffee.

"I am protecting myself. I have worked too hard to let all this slip away from me. You are a good friend and I thought after you had taken one of those pills you'd be so sick you wouldn't press this investigation so hard."

Rios tapped the desk. "You better go do your surgery. I'll be around."

Doc rose from the chair and Rios noticed his hand. "Doc, what happened? I noticed on the way back from San Jaime that you burned it — your hand?"

"It hurts like hell under the surgical gloves. I'm not sure where it came from." The hand disappeared in the tweed suit jacket pocket.

Doc cautiously moved to the door. Rios raised his voice, "You got the medication for those hippies from the Mercantile, right?"

"What?"

"You picked up the medication from the Mercantile in the morning. It was neatly wrapped in leather and hide bundles. The bundles had empty bottles the hippies returned when you and Dan went to the Mercantile in the afternoon."

"You knew all along. How did you figure it out?"

"Simply by having you tailed. The green truck up on the ridge is my stand-by deputy Catrados. I have his full report here." Rios waved a piece of paper at Doc.

"You may even know what color my underwear is, Rios, you are sharp, very sharp. Be careful, don't cut yourself." Doc was out the door and gone.

Rios frowned. "How are Quintana and Doc related in this scam?"

There was a knock on the door. Carl stuck his head in, "Red is here."

"Carl, follow the Doc. When he is finished with his surgery, I want him back."

"Aye, Aye, Captain." Carl disappeared.

The rain had stopped. Grey clouds still hung heavy overhead. Doc and Carl were talking in the parking lot. Doc was laughing. All the world could hear his nervous laugh. Rios reached over and with his finger tips swung the window closed. The air was cold.

Rios pushed the window back open. His eye caught a glimpse of Uncle Tito motioning below. Rios nodded and pointed his nose to the Mexican Cafe across the street. Rios touched his watch with one finger, then raised it in the air. Uncle Tito nodded, started his truck and drove off. Rios shut the window.

Rios buzzed Carolyn on the intercom, "Have the hospital send us a report of the hours Doc keeps at the hospital. Also, I need to know if Doc prescribed any medication to Ray Hava anytime this year, or his wife for that matter. Carolyn, call the hospital and have Carl paged. Tell him to come on back to the station. We probably can find out more on Doc when he's not around to defend himself."

Rios' head throbbed. He reread Carolyn's report.

Rios buzzed Carolyn again, "Could you take Red into Carl's room and ask her to identify Juan's photo? Don't tell her about his death. Also, tell her about Juan's dope selling." He clicked off. His eyes closed and he put hands to his head. Minutes passed.

Suddenly, Carolyn knocked on the door, pushed it open.

"Captain, the bank just called. They had a hold-up."

Rios grabbed his stetson hat from the hat rack, pulled his blue jean jacket off the back of the chair, darted out of the room.

He stopped at the top of the stairs, "Tell Carl I'm already there." He was gone with the slamming of the door.

Rios parked the truck in the No Parking Zone and ran inside. Mr. Brusher was pacing in front of the Greek fountain in the lush green foyer.

"Mr. Brusher, let's go into your office." The silver grey carpet was thick. Expensive pottery lamps sat on a six foot long mahogany desk.

"We've never had a robbery before. Well, I haven't, but the bank has. When my Grandfather ran this bank it was robbed regularly. It was a cousin of the James Brothers, but they've all gone now." He glanced at Rios.

Brusher took a large wooden box from his desk, opened it, handed it to Rios. They both lit up at the same time.

"Any idea who it was?" Rios asked.

"We'll know as soon as Bobby comes back with the developed film. You can't have a bank without the cameras, did you know that?" His deep set brown eyes showed strain under bushy eyebrows.

Brusher was a light-hearted man and his good will had kept the bank going. He was shorter than Rios, plump, with red hair, black mustache and slight beard. He was a man who once told tales by the hour with a glass of ale in his hand. But not since he took over his father's bank.

Bobby appeared with the film under one arm and a projector in the other. "Here, it is as clear as day. I'll let you decide for yourselves. Hi, Captain. Good to see you."

Rios grunted. Bobby set up the projector and loaded the film. "Captain, would you get the curtains?" Brusher switched off the lights.

Carl stepped into the room as the machine started. The picture showed six rows of booths, three were open. Theresa Montoya was helping a customer with Gladys Roybal standing behind her. The camera slowly swung to the front door and back again.

Rios smiled when he saw the old doper from the Mervinstride Hotel walk in.

But there was something different. He had shaved, his suit was clean, pressed, neatly buttoned.

He walked over to Theresa and waited his turn. Then he grew anxious and went to the next booth. The camera swung around again to the front door. Then it moved to the booth with the old doper.

Rosa Gabaldon, the teller, talked to him for a few minutes, then she started to search around her, growing more agitated every moment.

"There he is. See that old man with Rosa. He's our bank robber." Bobby leaned over, touching the image projected on the wall.

Carl stood up. "You mean that old buzzard is robbing the bank?" Rios gave Carl a stern glance. Carl sat down.

Now Rosa pulled open her money drawer and took the money out, put it in an envelope, and handed it over. As the old doper turned, the camera picked up a bright object in his hand.

"Stop the film. Does that look like a real gun to you?" Rios asked.

Brusher squinted, "Do you think it's a phoney?" The idea was reasonable.

Rios pulled open the door, "Excuse me, where is Rosa now?"

Brusher waved at Bobby to turn off the machine, "She's in the back with our security guard. I'll show you." He took Rios to the back of the bank.

"Rosa, this is Captain Rios, he would like to ask you some questions?"

Rosa blushed, "Certainly." Rios approached her, "Did you see a gun?"

Rosa spoke firmly, "Yes, it was pointed right at me." Rios smiled, "Was it a real gun?"

Rosa sat down. She frowned, "I couldn't tell you. It was so frightening to have that thing pointed at me. He spoke so harshly. He was desperate."

Rios nodded, "Thanks, we'll talk to you later."

Rios made his way to Carl, who was standing in the front of the bank. "Carl, I know our man. I bet I know where he is. I bet he still has the money."

Carl jumped in the truck with Rios. "You know bank robbers?"

Rios nodded again, it helped his stiff neck, "Yes, this man I know well. He's desperate because his connection was killed."

"You mean Juan Vaquero?"

"That's the one. Now this old guy has no way to get the dope he needs. If he didn't get any by this morning he'll be a wreck soon."

Rios walked into the Mervinstride Hotel. Carl walked in ahead.

Rios banged on door number seven. No answer. The small woman with ragged brown hair and the housecoat came hurriedly out of the back room.

"What do you want, cop man?"

Rios put his finger to his mouth. The small woman went quiet and she approached them turning her head from side to side. Carl took her arm and led her into the foyer.

"Do you have a master key? We need to get into that room, there may be a bank robber in there?" He whispered carefully.

The small woman shook her head, "You, nobody, got to get into dat room without a warrant." She shoved her hands into her apron and walked off down the hall.

"Carl you stay here and keep an eye on this room, I'll go get the warrant."

*****

"Carolyn, get the Judge on the phone for me, please. It's an emergency."

Carolyn grabbed the phone, "You find the bank robber yet?" Rios mumbled, "Esquibel, or Espinoza, I can't quite remember the man's name. He was in on charges of DWI about three months ago. It's strange the way life goes. I just spoke to him this morning."

"The Judge is on, use your phone."

Rios left the Judge's office and arrived at the Mervinstride Hotel just as Carl was stepping outside.

"Where are you going?"

Carl coughed, "Out for fresh air." Rios pointed inside, "You can get that later, let's go find that woman."

Rios banged on the door. The big woman in men's clothing had no clothing on now, except a man's bathrobe.

"What do you want?"

Rios stepped back, "We have a warrant to search Number Seven."

The big woman slammed the door.

Carl swallowed a cough, "I'd just as soon kick the damn door down, than go through this."

Seconds later, the big woman opened the door again, this time in a pair of men's pants, and a man's t-shirt with no sleeves. Carl turned and walked away.

From somewhere in the distance a phone rang. The big woman bellowed out, "Belle get that, could be important."

There was a scuffle behind them as the small woman squeezed by in a red bathrobe. The big woman knocked on Number Seven. No response. She put the key in the lock, mumbling to herself, and shoved the door open.

Rios and Carl carefully pushed past her. There on the bed lay the old doper. He had on the same suit he wore to the bank. His boots were next to him. The room had been ransacked. Carl put his hand on Rios' shoulder, pointing to the bottom of the old doper's feet. The socks on both feet had the bottoms neatly cut out. The flaps hung down. "That's a new MO."

Rios turned him over. He was dead, his throat slit. Blood had soaked into the bed, running down onto the dirty worn brown carpet, and staining the pillow lying on the floor.

"Oh, my God." The big woman escaped and ran down the hall. Carl darted after her.

"Wait a minute, we need to ask you some questions." The big woman stopped in her tracks. "Can I get my girlfriend to sit with me?"

Carl glanced around, "Where is she?"

A quiet answer, "In the bus depot." Carl saw the small woman sitting on the stool smoking a long thin cigar.

"Sure, just stay put."

"Here's the gun. You were right. It's silver coated plastic. How did you know?" Rios took it from Carl and dumped it into a plastic pouch.

"Just a hunch. Do you remember that old man who stopped all the cars driving by San Jaime and charged them a dollar to drive on the reservation to get to Tiwo Pueblo?"

"Yea, he was using a plastic badge from T.G. & Y. and a plastic gun."

Rios sighed. "It was hard to arrest someone with that great of an imagination. Carl, what's that on the floor?" Carl bent down, picked up a bottle.

Rios dropped it into the plastic pouch. "Carl, I'm going to give you a breather. Go and check the fingerprints on these. I have a hunch who we're after."

Rios handed Carl the satchel full of pouches. Carl took it gladly, "You mean that you are going to stay in this sweet rotten-grape-environment and interrogate the two lovelies?"

Rios slapped him on the back. "Get out of here. This place is tarnishing your sense of humor."

Rios closed the door, making sure it wasn't locked. He spoke to the two women, "Could I use your phone?" The two pointed to the desk in the bus depot. Rios strolled over and dialed.

"Carolyn, we have another body here at the Mervinstride. It's our bankrobber. Would you call the bank and talk to Brusher. We'll get the money as soon as we find the culprit that did this poor old man in. His name is Frank Esquibel."

Rios leaned over the counter. "We need a doctor for the autopsy. Maybe we should call in Mitch, again, he may be able to give us some fresh insight."

Carolyn whispered into the phone, "Rios, Doc is here. He showed up just a few minutes ago. He said you told him to come back after his surgery. What shall I do with him?"

"Send him on his way. I'll contact him later. I give him an E for effort."

"All right, hold on. I've got some information for you. Let me tell Doc he can leave."

Rios could vaguely make out the conversation. He smiled. They had paid extra for a phone with two lines and a hold button but Carolyn never used it. Rude, she said.

Rios noticed the note pad. Alex Cruz's name was on it and a telephone number. He copied it down on his note pad.

"Captain, Doc did not give out any prescription to Mr. or Mrs. Hava. Although he did recommend Hava to take gelatin vitamin E capsules for a bad burn on his arm. It was to stop the scarring. That was three months ago."

"Good, anything else?"

"Rios, why did you tell Doc that Catrados was the hot follower that came up with the evidence?" Carolyn sounded upset.

"Carolyn, I did that to make Doc nervous. He doesn't know who is following him and who isn't. I don't want him to be suspicious of you. You're supposed to be a good guy."

Carolyn's voice calmed, "A good guy? Oh, all right, I always wanted to be one of those; do I get a white hat?"

"Did Carl give you the prints to check?"

"Yes, and put Alex Cruz's name on them. Alcala gave him the name right off."

"Carolyn, call Mitch, send him over on this one. The bank needs to be notified about their robber. I'll see you soon. Be careful over there."

The women were whispering to each other as Rios talked. They were perched on the green couch like two pigeons at roost, holding hands and glaring.

"Well, who would like to tell me what happened?" Rios sat down on a dirty red banco that faced them. The two women stared at the floor.

"When did the old doper get back from the bank? And what was his name?" Rios held his knee and rocked back.

"His name was Frank Esquibel, you know that." The big woman firmly replied. Rios watched them.

Suddenly the little woman stood up, "I can't take dis pressure. You want to know what's going on here? Well, I'll tell ya. This Vaquero guy breaks in our place and kicks da bucket, den Oldie Esquie he goins nutso. He wants dis and he wants dat, den he goes and buys himself a plastic gun job. He is un nutty. He starts shakin' my Betsy here, and callin' us names, like we was somethin' different. We ain't no different from any man."

She pulled her robe tightly around, "He comes back from de bank with his socks bulging, carrying his boots. We laugh at him, he look da craziest ever. We never tink dat he has money in his socks! He call some kid from da school, da one with da pretty feathers in his hair. Now dat's strange, I only call da guys wid da feathers nuttsy. Da kid come runnin' over here like he was all hot. Da Esquie let him in, day were laughin' and like dat. Now old Esquie is dead."

She sighed and held out her hand to Betsy, "How we gonna keep da place open wid everyone here kickin' da bucket." She crumpled onto the couch. Big

Betsy put her arms around her and kissed her.

The ambulance arrived. The orderly held the door open. ''Where's the stiff? Mitch wants us to take it to the morgue. It's cleaner there.''

''He's in there.''

Rios then turned to the women, ''You can go now, thank you. If I should need any further information I will call before I come.''

They stumbled to their feet.

''That man should wear a shirt.'' The orderly nudged his chin towards Big Betsy. Rios smiled, she did fool some, strange it was the orderly.

The body was loaded onto the stretcher and Esquibel was carried out. Rios put the drawers back in the bureau, and gave the room one last searching glance. The money was gone. The boy with the feathers, Alex Cruz, would have some explaining to do.

* * * * *

''Well, what did you come up with?'' Rios threw his jacket on the table next to Carl's work bench.

Carolyn handed him the papers. Unidentified drug in the throat culture. ''Humm, as Mitch would say.'' Rios rubbed his chin.

* * * * *

The ground vibrated with the stampeding of bodies laden with drums, bells, heavy weight. Bells rang with each thrust of the ankles. Gourds heaved and rattled as dark arms covered with ash thrust their way forward. Chanting cut the still air like a sharp blade dripping blood. The sounds brought colors to mind.

Reds, yellows, greens, blues woven in the kilts of cotton embroidered with storm patterns. Pinon branches were wrapped in long strands of hair that flopped to the side of the head. Bracelets of wrapped wool billowed forward as the wrists gave warning jabs in the air.

The chanting became louder, the drums overwhelming, the world was closing in. Nee-nee pulled the blanket around her shoulders. She reached down and grabbed one of the pups that had strayed from the basket. Now the death cry was starting. Great whoops and cat calls danced through the air.

Under the covers the pup was warm and soft. ''I love you little fella. It's all right, stay still and close your eyes. The Indians are angry. When they're angry they go around and tell everyone. You don't want to see them. They have white faces, red arms, and they scream and yell frightening yells. They will not hurt us.''

Nee-nee gave the pup her finger to chew. She held her breath. The chanting had slowed, the drum was beating a steady rhythm.

"I wish I knew where I belong. There is this feeling inside of me, it hurts sometimes, it burns. Uncle Tito is my family, but where are those who would swim an ocean to find me. Does anyone ever have family who would give everything to be with them? Growing up is hard."

Footsteps were coming to the house: hurried, confused. They stopped at the door. She heard a soft knocking. The door groaned open. The board that was used to lock the door was lying next to the banco. The air blew across the blankets that hid her.

The drums were beating more rhythmically now, their sound in the distance down by the river.

"Nee-nee, it's me, Dan. Where are you?"

"What are you doing here?"

"They told me you'd been wounded, that police came and took you away to jail. I was worried. Then my sister told me a police woman had left a note for me. Why are you here? The uprising is coming?"

Nee-nee stared at him, drums were moving in closer now, the vibration increasing.

Dan mouthed 'let's go'. They eased under the bed and Dan slipped his arm around Nee-nee, his nose buried in her long hair. The drummers had split up and were moving around the house to the front. Someone was drumming on the door.

Dan held his breath, then let it out slowly.

Soft steady footsteps entered and moved into the kitchen. There was a loud noise, then another. No one would notice the hiding room unless they made a sharp right turn. There were no windows.

Voices in the kitchen. Someone else came in. Something fell, someone picked it up, replacing it.

They could hear the undertones of a heated conversation. The noise moved to the door, it creaked and the drums moved slowly away.

All was quiet. Dan rested his head back on the floor and breathed deeply. Minutes passed into hours and the hours disappeared into deep sleep.

* * * * *

"Cap, Red's still here. Want to see her?" Carolyn knocked on the lab door. Rios waved his hand, his attention on the microscope. Carolyn came in and closed the door. "What is it?"

"The stuff we got from the pharmacy, do you have the list handy?"

"Yes, it's on file."

"Let me see it. First I better talk with Red. Poor lady has enough tragedy in her life. Put the file on my desk." Rios stood up and took the tops off the petri dishes lined up on the black lab table.

"What's in there?" Carolyn pointed to the green matter growing in the petri dishes.

"Bacteria. The booze in the bottles we found in the Hotel rooms has a very heavy odor. I tried the contents out on these bacterial stains. The fluid kills the bacteria instantly."

Carolyn held up a dish. The bacteria was burned and black. "My God, just think what that stuff would do to human tissue."

"Exactly. Let's get going. Where's Red?" Rios put the dishes back into a white porcelain cupboard.

"In the office. Suppose that's where Doc got his burn? You did say he didn't have it when you drove him to San Jaime."

Rios smiled as he went into the office.

"Red, would you like some coffee?"

Red smiled, all teeth and gums. Rios walked over to the coffee maker.

"Red, did you know a man called Juan Vaquero?" Rios turned around handing her a mug. "Well, did you?"

Red tasted the coffee, "This isn't bad for a man." She smiled again.

"Red, I'm asking you this because something has happened to Juan."

"What has happened?"

"He's dead."

Red choked, the coffee spilled on her calico dress. Rios reached for a napkin.

Rios wiped her hand, wrinkled and red. She pulled away. "No, you're trying to trick me. You want me to tell you about the dopers."

Rios threw the soiled napkin in the trash. "No, I know all about the dopers. When did you last see Juan?"

"You don't think I did it do you?"

Rios put his hand on her shoulder, "No, I know who killed him."

Red sat on the straight wooden chair. "First Ray Hava and now Juan Vaquero. Why?" Red burst into tears, her whole body heaving.

Rios pulled open the bottom drawer of his desk and handed her a white box of tissue. "Red, what did Ray and Juan have in common?"

"They were both good men. They tried hard to get ahead and they both were afraid of Cruz."

Rios sat down at the desk. "Cruz? What about Cruz?"

"They both knew about him and the San Thomas woman. They knew if they talked they would be in trouble. But Cruz was never quiet, he always bothered them. The only person who knew the true story and kept it to himself was Uncle Tito. Cruz could never find anything in Uncle Tito to hold over him."

Red closed her eyes, "Juan and I were together last night. The Hotel had a room with a broken window, we were in there. It was my last . . . piece of

Heaven. We were going to get married and get out of here."

"Red, when you and Juan were in that room with the broken window, was the gas on from the stove?"

Red shook her head, "We had to meet on the sly, my old boyfriend still stays there. The gas, no."

"Red, did your old boyfriend know what you were doing last night?"

"I doubt it. He passes out around sundown. That's why I left him. He was so full of doper and booze by six o'clock I didn't have any fun with him. I like to dance and socialize. After being at work behind a hot stove all day, I like to go out at night. No, I don't think Frank knew we were there."

Rios sighed and held his head, "Red, who would want Juan dead?"

"It's obvious, isn't it? Cruz wants him dead, Cruz wants everyone dead. The only thing I could never figure out was what he was doing with the woman from San Thomas. She's married, happily, and has a good business."

"Do you know a man just in from Arizona?" Rios tried a long shot.

Red smiled, "That drives a silver Cadillac and wears fancy city clothes?"

"Something like that, yes." Rios stood up.

"Someone who might have come from Phoenix?"

"Could be, do you know this person?"

"No."

Rios stood at the window. His back to Red, he raised his voice. "Red, Frank Esquibel is dead, too. He robbed a bank, took the money to the Hotel, and was found dead."

"Oh, my God." Red rocked back and forth on the chair and the chair groaned with her. "I want to go home."

Rios whispered, "Sure. Be careful, keep in touch." He didn't move. Red pounded her way down the hall.

Rios straightened his desk, pulled out a cigarette, unlit he put it to his lips, breathed in heavily, then put it back in the pack.

He glanced at his watch. Almost one o'clock.

Carolyn was changing the typewriter ribbon as Rios walked down the hall. "Carolyn, what did Mitch say about the autopsy?"

Carolyn picked up a piece of paper. "Here, he dropped this off. He worked fast. Funny how he smelled of gas. Oh, and here's the report from the pharmacy."

Rios took the paper, "Please call Marge for me and tell her I won't be in for lunch or that nap."

Carolyn raised her eyebrow.

* * * * *

Death by strangulation, cause unknown. Gas fumes were not in the man's lungs. So he was dead before the gas was turned on. The man had no alcohol in his stomach, not for the last ten hours anyway, and he would let Rios know about the drugs after a blood test.

The buzzer sounded on Rios' desk. He picked up the phone, opened his mouth to speak. "Captain Rios, this is the secretary of the Medical Board. Since you need a doctor who is licensed and able to work, we are sending out to you Dr. Griffith. He can replace Doctor Tapia if need be. Please do not allow Doctor Mitchell to work on any medical cases. He has been stripped of his license to practice and has no legal authority to write a prescription." The phone clicked.

Rios walked back down the hall. "That was the Medical Secretary, she says they are sending out another doctor by the name of Griffith. Let him get in touch with Mitch. They probably have a lot in common. I'm going out."

Rios swung his blue jean jacket over his shoulder, "Any news on Carl and Alex?"

Carolyn shook her head.

The wind blasted against his face as he walked to the Mexican Cafe. The waitresses would be in a stew over Juan and Red.

Uncle Tito's truck was parked down the street in front of the hardware store and Uncle Tito motioned to Rios. He crossed the street and followed him back into the alley.

"What's up?" Rios pulled his jacket collar around his chin. Uncle Tito scanned the alley.

"The drugs are in the leather hides and pelts. I found some that Doc dropped down by the river."

Rios nodded, "We found out about that."

Uncle Tito pulled a photo out of his pocket and handed it to Rios. Rios stared at it in disbelief.

Uncle Tito put his hand into a glove, winked at Rios, "Hot stuff, huh?" Rios' eyes were frozen on the photo. When he looked up Uncle Tito had disappeared. The photographer must have been Cruz.

Rios headed for the office. "Carolyn, we need a search warrant for a house on the Pueblo-town border, call Judge Trujillo and see if he could get it. It's urgent."

Rios walked up to his desk, pulled a cigarette out of the pack and lit up this time.

*****

Carl parked next to the school bus in front of the school and pushed the handcuffs down inside the back of his pants. The school was quiet, classes were in session. He walked down the long hall to the principal's office.

"Well, well, well, if it's not the police. Are you here for a demonstration or to arrest someone?" The black man with a high forehead shook Carl's hand.

Carl frowned, he hated to be second guessed. "I'm here to find Alex Cruz, do you know where his class is?"

The principal pointed down the hall and they walked together to the classroom. The teacher waved them in.

Alex half stood up at his seat. His pockets bulging. The principal motioned him down but he suddenly ran for the door. Two other boys blocked him halfway up the aisle. Carl handcuffed him and led him out into the hall.

"You're coming with me, renegade."

Alex shoved against him, "My Dad won't like you calling me names. Watch it."

"You can have long conversations with dear old Dad in City Jail. Move it."

Old Baker met them at the entrance of the jail.

"Got another one for me, do you?" Old Baker took Alex into the complex. Alex didn't give Old Baker a hard time. He was six feet and weighed two hundred pounds of pure muscle. Old Baker had once been up for the middle weight championships and had his pictures in the papers — they were now all over the jail. No one had ever escaped from Old Baker.

Rios met Carl on the stairs of the Police Station, "Carl, can I go with you back to the jail to interrogate Cruz?"

Carl frowned, "Don't you have that backwards? Don't you want me to go with *you* to the jail, isn't that the way it goes?"

Rios put his hat on, "If you like, thanks, I'd love to." Carl drove.

Rios turned to Carl, his hat touching the ceiling of the Pontiac, "Did you frisk Alex?"

"Yes, and you won't believe what I found. Something I haven't seen around here before." Carl reached into his coat pocket and pulled out six sandwich bags of white powder.

"Impressive stuff. Heroin?"

"Yup, the white poison, itself. Where do you suppose the kid got all that stuff?"

"Do you remember the kaleidoscope factory calling in last week. There was a fight between Doc's boy and some fancy dressed stranger?"

"I took the call. You were still out cold. They said Doc's boy hit the city guy across the backside with a two-by-four. Knocked him out. No one had seen him before. Wonder what he was doing in the back of the Mercantile. The only way back there is the key Quintana had around his neck."

Rios lit up a cigarette, "Carl, this Hava death is bringing out everybody's bad traits. There sure seems to be a lot coming to the surface. And the Hava woman still bothers me."

Carl pulled up in front of the jail. Old Baker opened the car door for Rios.
"We're seeing a lot of Carl lately. Is it his turn to stay this time?"

Rios hunched his sore shoulder. "We're here to visit your house guests,
which way?" Old Baker led Rios down the hall to the end. The jail could hold
twelve prisoners.

"Hello, Cruz. Time for a talk?" Rios pulled up a bench from the outside wall.
Cruz turned his back on Rios and stared out the window.

"Cruz, we got your son on two charges of murder." Cruz grunted.

"But you know that already, don't you?"

Cruz turned. "Rios, what you think and what you do is your business. I don't
give a damn. You wouldn't take my advice, you want to be a smart ass, go
ahead. Things happened the way they did 'cause you interfered. Get the hell out
'a here." He straightened his back, his nostrils flared.

"Cruz, where did Alex get the heroin?" Rios pulled the bags out of his
pocket.

"Like hell, man. My son never did heroin, head poison, that stuff's pure crap,
he never did heroin and you know it. If he did it would be all over this small
hole-of-a-town." Cruz spat on the floor.

Rios pushed his hat back, "This is heroin and it has your son's prints all over
it. We found it on him when he was arrested at school. Do you know the charges
for possession and selling of heroin on school property?"

"Hell, that's a lie and you know it. My son is too damn clever to get into that
stuff. You planted it and I can prove you did."

"Cruz, do you know who killed Hava?"

Cruz grabbed the bars, "Rios, you ain't gettin' nothin' out of me, 'cept a hard
time, now get lost." He walked back to the window.

They drove back to the station. Rios picked up the envelope on his desk. The
search warrant for Cruz's house was in it. His next stop. Under the envelope was
a letter from the county jail in Alcala. Quintana was being held without bail. Mary
Quintana was discharged on a ten thousand dollar bail bond note.

* * * * *

Uncle Tito walked into the dark room. He picked up a chair and pounded it
on the floor with a loud thump. Dan rolled from under the bed, his mouth open,
his hands up. Nee-nee grabbed the pup ready to fight.

"Uncle Tito, they were here. The Clan, they came. They were in the kitchen."
Uncle Tito turned and ran into the kitchen.

He threw up his hands. "They took my stuff. It was going to be evidence for
the police."

Dan sat on the edge of the bed. "They must have known you had it."

Uncle Tito placed one finger on Dan, "Do you know Gerald?" Dan nodded. "We're both students in the special education program."

"He probably told. His uncle is in the Clan."

Uncle Tito sat down. "What are you doing here, Dan?"

Dan walked over to the door, "I was worried about Nee-nee and I brought her stuff."

Uncle Tito patted Nee-nee, "Get your things on. I'll take Dan into the kitchen for some coffee."

As they stepped over the mother dog, Uncle Tito reached down and felt her belly. He frowned, "Dan, we better move her outside. She's dead."

* * * * *

Rios put the warrant on the seat. It might not hold up in court but it would get him into the house to find evidence that would. He drove through the Pueblo and over the bridge.

The house was dark.

Rios walked over to the shed. The door hung on one hinge. Rios put his hand on top of the mud roof and peered inside.

Burlap bags were piled on top of each other. Rios grabbed the bag on top and grain poured out. Rios wiped his hands on his blue jeans.

The screen door of the main house fell into his hands as he touched the door handle. Rios leaned it against the adobe wall. The front door handle was stiff. Rios stood on his toes and peered into the living room. Suddenly his hand touched something on the window sill, the key.

The front door pushed open to an overwhelming stench. That was it, the smell: the smell in Hava's bedroom was not his imagination.

His eyes absorbed the mess in the room. Ashes from a fire were in the middle of the mud floor, black char on the ceiling. The far right corner had a banco built to go around the corner of the room.

Rios pulled the photo out of his pocket; there was the banco. An old Navajo blanket in tatters lay covered with bottles of vodka, the same brand found in the Mervinstride victims' rooms. To the left was a small doorway. The window straight ahead was broken, glass all over the floor. Alex's feather collection and dancing kilt lay on the floor, on top of the broken glass.

Rios kicked a beer can out of the way and walked into the room on his left. There were niches on the inside wall. One held a tall bottle with a poison sign on it. The other had a rodent's skull. Rios held the photo up, the same skull was in the photo.

He stepped down, to his right was a long metal table covered with photographic equipment. There was a clear space with a poster-size photo lying upside down. Rios eased it over.

"My God, what a mind," he was appalled. Rios moved to the window. The photograph was a full length image of Juan Vaquero with the San Thomas woman. They were posed nude in a graphic embrace. Their wrinkled out-of-shape bodies grasped each other in emotion. Or was it?

Rios rolled it up, put it under his arm. He turned to go around the table but his boot kicked something. There below the table was a vat of dark yellow fluid.

Rios squatted down, smelled it, a sweet oily smell — the same as the Hava bedroom smell. He pulled a vial from his pocket, filled it. The stuff burned his hands, he wiped it off on his pants. It bleached his blue jeans.

"I wonder if this is the same fluid Alex offered his friends to drink."

Rios moved around the table. There was another poster, this one of Hava. Another project of poor taste. Hava was standing behind a fire in the front room, no clothes, full frontal display.

What was this? Did these people do this willingly, or did Cruz blackmail them into doing it? Rios rolled it up and pushed it under is arm with the other.

"Time to get out of here."

Rios picked up some bottles, paper, tongs, and a small box filled with chemicals and put the pouches of evidence into the truck.

* * * * *

"Carolyn, is Carl back yet?" Carolyn swallowed the last of her cookie, "Yes, he came back empty-handed. He's in the print room."

Rios went into his office and put the photos on his desk. "Carl, could you come in here a moment?"

Carl came in carrying a petri dish, "What did you find?"

Rios pulled his jacket off carefully, "Well, I got a lot of things that need your going over." Rios unloaded his pockets and lifted the plastic vial with the yellow fluid in it. "This is the stuff we smelled in Hava's room. Find out what it is and be careful, it burns everything it touches."

"But wait a second, there's more. Close the door." Rios unrolled a photo and held it up to Carl.

"What in the world? Where did you find that?" Rios chuckled, "Wait, what do you think of this one?" He held up the picture of Vaquero and the woman.

Carl sat down. "She looks better with her clothes on. What are these for?"

"I don't now, I was thinking of asking Cruz himself in the morning. Meanwhile we better keep these locked up in the safe. Do you think you could check out that yellow stuff tonight, and let me know what it is?"

Carl held the vial up to the light, "I bet I can guess. This was with his photographic stuff?"

Rios nodded pulling out a cigarette. "Yeah, can I smoke around it?"

Carl turned the vial, "Sure, but not too close. This is developing solution. It's dangerous stuff. I'll find out for sure and let you know."

Rios sat down in his chair, "I'm going home after I make a phone call, so if you find out anything call me at home."

Carl turned, "The new Doc, Doctor Griffith, is here. He called right after you left. I may call him in for an opinion on this." Carl waved the vial and left the room.

Rios put his feet up on the desk and called home, "Marge, how are things? What a day. I'll be glad to get home to you and a nice warm meal. Do you still have that book on Indian magic?" Rios blew the smoke out of his mouth, "Okay, see you in a few minutes."

Rios glanced at his watch, a quarter to five. He put on his hat and jacket walking down the hall. Carolyn had left. There was a note on her desk: Pick up Floyd Custer at four-thirty at the bus depot. What a place to arrive, it would give Floyd an eye opener to the town.

Floyd Custer might stir up some interest, Rios could give him reservation duty. Rios laughed, that would put the rookie through his paces.

Rios opened the wall safe and threw in the photos, closed the heavy door, and flipped out the light.

*****

The pups whimpered, searching for something to feed their hunger. Nee-nee picked them up and put them in one of Uncle Tito's large baskets and carried them into the kitchen. She pulled out the honey jar and fed them by sticking her little finger into the honey and putting it up to each waiting mouth.

Uncle Tito stamped the mud off his boots as he entered the kitchen. "Nee-nee, I'm taking Dan back to town. Lock the door this time." He pointed to a two-by-four to place across the back door. "They got what they came for, I don't think they'll be back." Uncle Tito disappeared.

Nee-nee fed the puppies with honey, and then goat's milk, and tucked them into the basket with an old bathrobe that belonged to someone from long ago.

She thought back to what Dan had said, "Her parents were coming from a far away land." How far away? She didn't even remember her mother, well maybe a little. It hurt not to be able to remember her face. The nights of crying and screaming — wanting her mama.

The pups would forget their mama, too. Her mother was beautiful. The excuse her Grandma gave was it would be a good experience for Nee-nee to stay with Uncle Tito. Uncle Tito had helped her dad once. Her dad helped Uncle Tito with something. That something must have been a lot.

But she could remember him. He was tall with a thin line mustache. He wore silk suits and black patent leather shoes. She used to sit on the bed watching him polish them. He would ask if she could see herself. They would laugh. He was fun. Her mama and dad were happy together. Then something happened, they sent her away.

The only vision Nee-nee could remember was sitting in her mom's lap while they drove to the airport. Her mother had on white gloves, a pearl necklace and a light grey-blue chiffon dress. Her mother held her so tightly Nee-nee could hardly breathe. Her mother was singing "The Fox," her father would join in the chorus. Nee-nee had felt safe in her mother's firm hug. Then everything changed.

Nee-nee closed her eyes, searching her memory for a vision of her mother's face. There was none.

The puppies started to whine and wiggle. "I'm staying around until you're full grown and big enough to remember me." She picked up the basket and hummed.

She was seven and a half when this mud house had become her home and life. She was sixteen in July. Nine years of her life had been with Uncle Tito, only seven and a half with her parents. Nee-nee closed her eyes and leaned back.

Suddenly, Nee-nee put the basket aside and moved quietly to the front door. Two men were quarreling.

"I found her, I want her back!"

"You no longer have any hold on her. Leave."

"Uncle Tito, this was not meant to go so far. I tried to send money, we tried to find you."

"If you tried so hard, then why didn't you?"

"Believe me, I tried. Mailing money isn't easy. I couldn't just send it to a General Delivery address with a Pueblo full of drunks!"

"Sam, you never tried or it would have come. She cried out for you and you never answered. I mailed her letters, they didn't come back. Where did they go?"

"We, I . . . I got the letters, Elizabeth is dead. She died four months after . . . after . . . after we sent Diana here. She never saw Europe."

"Sam, you've been gone almost nine years. She's given up the hurt she felt, don't hurt her again."

Nee-nee opened the door. Uncle Tito was standing with his back against the door frame. A man in a shiny silk suit with black patent leather shoes stood facing him. Tears streaked down his face, pooling on creases in his frown. Suddenly Uncle Tito noticed Nee-nee. The man moved slowly to her.

"Diana, It was supposed to be different." He wiped his face with a white handkerchief. "It was supposd to be happy." He folded the handkerchief putting it back in his suit pocket.

Nee-nee touched the creases in his face.

"I came when I heard you were in trouble. I came right away. I just arrived. Oh, Diana, my Diana."

"My name is Nee-nee."

"Can I come in?"

She led him through the front room into the kitchen. Uncle Tito sat on a bench in the corner. He picked up his willow strands, working on basket. Nee-nee put everything away and then ladled water from a bucket sitting in the mud sink into a pan and blew on the wood fire in the cooking stove. The water boiled in the silence of three people lost in their own thoughts. Nee-nee added some herbs to the boiling water and poured it into mugs.

"You were the man Dan hit, weren't you?"

"Yeah, I was. I had seen your head pop out two or three times. I asked Quintana whose head it was . . . he said probably yours. He let me in the back to surprise you. That's some boyfriend you've got. Must be true love."

Uncle Tito grunted. Nee-nee watched her father. No one had said so much in the mud house before. Her father talked with a funny accent.

"It was a matter of life and death." She stopped. Uncle Tito had taught her that fewer words were better than many. She realized her feelings toward him were different, now that he was a real person.

"Let's go for a drive in my Cadillac. How 'bout it?"

"Sure."

Uncle Tito didn't look up as they left the house. They drove through the Pueblo and into Jerez without speaking.

"You hungry?"

"The Mexican Cafe, it's got good chili."

"Okay, point it out."

The cafe was full of locals, it was just after five o'clock. The workers were coming into town for dinner.

Nee-nee noticed the waitresses were red-eyed, quiet.

"Jumping joint in the big town, huh?" Sam remarked looking around him. Nee-nee frowned, "Excuse me, I'll be back." She walked to the ladies' room in the back. She hadn't let her father know Uncle Tito just had an outhouse. It embarrassed her, yet Uncle Tito refused to have a bathroom in the house. He thought it was unhealthy and unnecessary.

"Red, what's the matter?" She was sitting on the toilet with the top down. The large body heaved in sobs.

"Juan Vaquero is dead, Esquibel is dead, and Ray Hava, too."

Nee-nee knelt beside her on the spotless white linoleum floor. "Do you know who did it?" Red gulped for air, layers of pain rippling through her body.

"Alex Cruz. He killed Old Esquie and bought smack dope with the poor sweet man's money."

"There is no smack around here. It's all in Alcala." Red blew her nose, "No, girl, there's a fancy man in fancy dress clothes selling hard smack here. He came up a week ago from Phoenix."

Red shook her head, "I'm gonna sell this dump and go to California. Just watch me. This is a lonely life, girl, it only get's lonelier." Red heaved up her body and waddled out the door.

Nee-nee stood thinking. the man sounded like dad. If he had been here all this time, why did he decide to appear this afternoon?

* * * * *

"Captain, this is Red. I hate to bother you at home, but you know the man in the fancy suit? He's here. Carey says he's ordered dinner. Carey talked to him and he got here last week from Phoenix . . . Sure thing, Captain."

Red hung up and reached out her long wrinkled red hands and grabbed two waitresses.

"Flirt with the man. Make him to home. Rios wants us to keep him occupied 'till he gets here." She let them go smiling, "I ain't dead yet."

Nee-nee came out of the ladies' room. Red waved to her as she passed the steamy kitchen. Carey, the petite waitress was talking to her dad, twirling her long black hair around her finger and smiling out of the side of her mouth.

Nee-nee went to the table, pulled out a chair and gracefully fell into it. Two could play this game. Carey gave Nee-nee a too-sweet smile and left for the kitchen.

"Nice joint for a small town. Real friendly around here." Nee-nee stared at him. He was different than she remembered, very different.

"Now it's my turn. I drove all the way from Phoenix. Better relieve myself before the beer gets here." He gave a chuckle, pushing in his chair, slicking back his hair.

Nee-nee stared at her hands. Phoenix, Red said he's been here a week. Dan smacked him days ago.

The lights of passing cars shined across her face. Wind blew the street lamps casting a blurred light back and forth across her face. Tumbleweeds, papers, dirt flew hard against the windows. She moved her water glass to the other side and slid into the opposite chair. Now her back was to the front door and she was facing the kitchen. She heard her father laugh and looked up.

Carey and her father were entwined against the men's room door. He pinched her, she giggled. His hand was placed firmly on her hips. Nee-nee noticed the people next to her pointing at them. Nee-nee covered her eyes with her hand.

"Hello, Diana, sorry to be so long. I was detained. I like your little town. Say, when do we eat?" Nee-nee kept her hands over her eyes.

"No sooner said than done," Carey put the bowls of chili on the table. Carey's hand squeezed Nee-nee's shoulder. Nee-nee pulled away.

"Come on, what's the matter, let's eat." Her father handed her a spoon. "I can remember feeding you oatmeal. Most of it landed in my lap, or on my shoes." He lifted his foot. They were still there — black patent leather shoes.

Nee-nee slowly ate her chili. Doc Tapia's influence had come in handy, she could eat, listen, and think all at once. "Dad, what happened to my mother?"

Sam froze, his spoon half way up to his mouth. "Your mother?"

"Yes, where is she?"

Sam put the spoon down and took a gulp of beer. "Diana, your mother had a lot of problems. She was very sick when we sent you away. She didn't want you to know, she wanted to get well and live her life with you." He watched the car lights float by outside. "She isn't coming back." His pale face peered out through layers of sad tears. He touched Nee-nee's arm. "I loved that woman."

The front door opened and no one walked past them. She was going to turn, find out why, when Red came up.

"Hello, fat mama, the table's full."

The color had returned to Sam's face. His sadness turned to anger at the interruption.

"Nee-nee, could I show you some fine hot sopapillas? You pick the ones you want to take home, okay?" Red smiled.

"Fat broad, get lost!" Sam shouted.

Red put her red wrinkled hand out and Nee-nee took it. "Sure, I'd love to." Sam threw his spoon into the chili bowl. It splattered on his shiny suit.

"Things will change when I get you home, young lady, no respect." He grabbed his napkin as Red led Nee-nee to the back of the kitchen. She sat her down on a stool.

"Here, put this on." Red handed Nee-nee an apron. "You can make your own."

"I can drop them into the hot grease and watch them puff up?"

Red wiped her leaking eyes, "Yes, now here's the batter and the tongs."

Nee-nee threw her arms around Red. "I love you, Red. I think you're beautiful."

A waitress leaned over the service counter and whispered loudly, "Red, I need that enchilada, green with an egg. The Captain is hungry. If he don't get it soon, he's gonna leave."

Red held Nee-nee in a tight hug. Nee-nee could hear Red's stomach gurgle and the soft crying sounds she made.

"God love ya, God love ya." Red said as she hugged the girl.

Red let go, "The grease is ready, let's drop the batter, grab the tongs." The two of them oblivious to the world around, forgetting the man at the table, cooked far into the evening.

In between sopapillas Red fixed Mexican plate specials, tacos, enchiladas. The food, grease and the evening faded slowly.

Nee-nee, startled, picked up the kitchen clock. "Red, it's almost midnight."

Nee-nee ran into the dining area. Everyone was gone, including her father.

"Red, that man sitting with me was my father."

"Looks like he's gone."

"Red, are we just empty creatures deceiving ourselves that some people really care? I mean, how do you know when someone says 'I love you' if they mean it or they are saying it 'cause it sounds good? Are we so desperate to fill our emptiness that we'll believe anyone in order to avoid being empty, even if we're deceiving ourselves?"

"We all need love. You sound as if it means tricking people or having people trick you?"

Nee-nee frowned, "Well, maybe that, too. Sometimes I feel the need to hug somebody, to give them some of my love, or I'll explode. Like tonight, we hugged. I know you are real. You feel, you care, you are honest in your giving. But sometimes I've thought people were honestly giving and it was just a deception. How do you know the difference between what they give and what you want?"

Red smiled. "Child, it comes with patience, hurt, lies, and fear. Believe in the feelings you give out and be honest with them. Leave the rest alone. Thinking too much isn't good for anybody. It confuses your heart. The empty feeling will fix itself. You don't need other folks to fill it — you do it."

Nee-nee put her hands up in the air to stretch. Red grabbed them, "Don't be disrespectful of your father. Everyone tries to make it the best waẏ they can." Nee-nee stared out the window.

The door vibrated with pounding. "A late customer. Thaṭ's what happens when you're too good." Red moved her large shape and opened the door. Rios stood there, hat in hand.

"Business has been taken care of. How are the sopapillas?" He winked at Red. She gave him a warm smile.

"My co-worker and I are finished. Just might keep her."

Red pulled off the grease-stained, flour coated apron. "Captain, since you're up and Nee-nee needs a ride home, could you take her?"

"Sure, be glad to."

Red packed up a large brown grocery bag filled with sopapillas, "Don't want you to go home empty handed after all that work." They went out and got into the truck.

The moon was a sliver in the sky. The world was quiet. The wind had stopped. Nee-nee stared out the window at the silhouettes, as the truck bounced down the dirt drive to Uncle Tito's house.

"Here we are. Nee-nee, go in and investigate. If everything checks out, wave to me from the front door. I do this with all my dates." Rios patted her hand. Nee-nee gathered up the large brown bag in her arms.

"Nee-nee?"

"Yes, sir?"

"What does Nee-nee mean?"

"Butterfly."

"That's nice, well, better get going, it's late."

Nee-nee stepped out of the truck into the black stillness and pushed her hair behind her neck. She slammed the truck door and ran into the house, leaving the house door open. She glanced into her room, the basket with the pups was gone. She darted into the kitchen, her moccasins silent on the hard mud floor.

In the kitchen, Uncle Tito was asleep in his big chair. His feet perched on top of the table, the basket with the pups lay at his side. They were all asleep. Nee-nee quietly put the brown bag on the wooden table, moved to the front door, and waved. Rios drove off into the night, a cigarette glowing in his mouth.

* * * * *

Marge held open the front door, her flannel nightgown buttoned to her chin. "Is she all right? Was Uncle Tito waiting for her?"

"She's all right, didn't see Uncle Tito."

Rios rubbed his hands together. The night air was frosty cold. "She didn't seem to know anything about her dad. Red handled it beautifully."

Rios kissed Marge on the forehead. "Red called Nee-nee back to the kitchen and they made sopapillas. Carl and I then asked Sam Cavilli to come with us outside. Carl had the handcuffs ready and we read him his rights and took him down to Old Baker."

Rios put his feet up on the stool next to the couch, "Before Old Baker took him in we got Sam to write down permission for us to open and search his car. Carl thought that one up. Sam really got worried. We allowed him his one phone call but he didn't want it."

Marge handed Rios a cup of tea. "Thanks, Hon, well, the back of the car was empty, the interior was clean, so, Carl pulled out his penknife and cut the back of the driver's seat. Wump, out it fell, enough smack to light up San Jaime for a year."

"What will happen to him?" Marge sipped her tea as she reached up and turned off the lamp over her head.

"Well, we'll move him to Alcala for the authorities there to handle. Quintana is there now, Alex will be moved." Rios put his tea cup down and took Marge's hand. "Come one, we can discuss this in a horizontal postion."

Marge set the tea cup on the edge of the coffee table, pushing it quickly to the center as Rios pulled her to his side.

"Doc will be next. He'll probably be let out on bond, although it depends on the type of dope he was pushing, if he was really pushing dope."

Marge settled on the bed, watching Rios undress. "Do you really think Doc is guilty?"

"I don't know. It's hard to believe a man who has done so much for our community has been driven that low. I wonder if there isn't something else behind all this." He slipped on his pajama bottoms, tossed his hat on the bed post, and slid into bed next to Marge.

"Why would he get involved with Quintana?" Marge stroked Rios' hair back from his face.

"The thing I can't figure on is Nee-nee's father showing up like that. The man never had a reason to come and get his little girl. Then out of the woodwork he comes. Not only bringing concern for his daughter, but a couple pounds of heroin. Where did he come from: Phoenix. Why did he come: to see his kid. Whatever for: who knows." Rios hugged Marge close to him.

"Do you think Doc called him to come get his daughter?" Marge stroked Rios' chest.

"No, somehow, it doesn't tie in. Doc would have no way of knowing who Nee-nee's parents are, unless through some medical records." Rios kissed Marge's hair. "Well, let's sleep on it." He reached over and turned off the lamp and pulled Marge to him. There was soft patter on the floor, then a heavy thump.

"Our chaperon has arrived."

"Good night, Moses." Rios gave him a soft kick as he rolled over.

Thursday: Day 7

The phone shook Rios awake. He grabbed the mouthpiece. "All right, what is it?"

"Rios, we got it."

"Got what?"

"Doctor Griffith and I have proof that the chemical you found killed Juan Vaquero. Alex confessed in the Alcala interrogation that his father showed him how to put the chemical into a gelatin capsule. When the capsule is placed in the mouth with water, it starts to disintegrate. The strong chemical inside and the water outside get the capsule to the throat or the esophagus. It sticks there due to the size of the capsule and the sticky structure of the gelatin capsule. The chemical then oozes out and slowly kills the victim. Cruz showed him how it worked before he gave it to Hava. They used this technique on their dog and some of the chickens. We went out this morning and found dead chickens and a dead dog wrapped in a burlap sack out back of the mud shed. Say Rios, when are you coming in?"

Rios turned the clock on the bedside table, a quarter to eleven.

"I'll be right there, just finishing some coffee." Carl chuckled, "It's all right, Captain. You need the rest. Things have been going full speed ahead and then some. Take your time." He hung up.

Marge rolled over, a warm smile on her face. "What's up?" Rios grabbed his boots, put his hat on his head, and headed to the bathroom. "Me. It's almost eleven."

He grabbed Marge's book on Indian magic that lay on the kitchen table, slammed the front door and jumped into the truck.

Rios went up the stairs two at a time. He smiled to himself thinking back to when he could hardly get one boot up the stairs at a time. Carolyn met him at the top of the stairs.

"Welcome, the night wanderer returneth."

Rios called the head of the Pueblo Council. They had been pressured by Cruz. Salazar was afraid to admit anything was going on in the Pueblo, but once Rios broke the news to him that the information was already out, the man talked.

They had been threatened by Cruz, and they weren't going to do or say anything one way or the other. They would wait for Rios to call them into court.

Rios hinted that if the Indian Council would cooperate, Evelyn Hava might get her money sooner. The Indian man's voice tensed. "Evelyn Hava is a good woman. We would not want to keep her in misery. We have nothing to say, that is all."

Rios should have known better to try a ploy on him. It only showed that Evelyn Hava was well protected by her people. Rios shook his head. It was hard to believe Cruz killed Hava. The day Cruz called Rios out, Cruz was worried, worried and nervous enough to try to find the real killer. If Cruz was the killer, he wouldn't have bothered Rios.

Rios opened Marge's book on Indian magic and thumbed through. There was a photo for each kachina doll. On the side was the definition of the different kachinas.

"Kachinas are not made by the river Pueblos. Kachinas are made by a certain tribe of Indians. Each kachina contains part of the spirit of the carver. The spiritual relationship of the carver and the kachina remain in harmony forever. If bad comes to the carver the kachinas will hold the carver's spirit until the evil is corrected. The restlessness of the carver lives on forever bringing bad luck to the holder of the kachina."

Rios thumped the page with his index finger. "Ah-ha." The buzzer on his desk lit up.

"Captain, it's Mary Quintana. Also, the guy from the garage, the one with the strange accent called in. The impounded car from the drive-in is leaking all over his lot. He wants it moved. Where shall we put it?"

"Tell him to call Jose at the Motor Division."

Rios picked up the phone. Mrs. Quintana wanted know if she came up with certain information would it help her husband in sentencing. Rios gave her a noncommittal answer, and hung up.

Rios remembered Doc's remark about the kachinas that Hava carved. He had traded for it and Hava's hearth was missing a kachina. Rios opened the book again.

He called the ZIA Police. Cruz hung around them, perhaps they were in on the take. But they refused to answer any questions. They would not appear in court, their reservation was private property. Rios' only reply was that they should take better care of it.

Carl stuck his head in, "Sir, we got it, pay dirt. Doc was being blackmailed for three grand. Cruz got a photo of him, too. I played along like we knew about it and Doc fell right into our hands."

There was a knock on the door. "I'll get it." Carl jumped up, "It's Doctor Griffith, he's going to help me work on writing up the capsule theory, and Floyd is here. Arrived last night with Carolyn picking him up at the Bus Depot. They've already struck up quite a friendship. She's a fast mover."

The phone rang, "Rios here." Carl disappeared out the door. Rios heaved a sigh and lit up a cigarette.

Mary Quintana had asked the employees at the Mercantile to help her find any evidence that would help weed out the killer. On the quiet, one employee, had told her that one of the kachinas Hava had carved for his wife was sitting in the ZIA Police Headquarters. Also, that Mrs. Hava had no money and was building up her credit. Mrs. Hava had explained that soon she would be able to get Hava's savings, once the trial was over. This morning a young woman, Doc's daughter, had come into the store and paid on Mrs. Hava's bill. She'd used another name which was strange since they all knew her. No one could understand a woman playing such a foolish game.

Mrs. Quintana cleared her throat, "They all admitted they owed Cruz money. He had "black knowledge" on some of them. If it wasn't a night out with someone else or a fictional reason it was something else that Cruz had over each of them. You work with people day in and day out and they still keep secrets from you."

She had to help a customer and rang off as Rios frowned, "The kachina, ten-to-one the savings are in the kachina." Marge had told Rios of an old lady who had come into the beauty parlor and told them how she had cleaned for the Governor of the Pueblo one year. He kept his life savings in the arms of a fat badger kachina. Everytime she picked it up to dust it, she got an eerie feeling like she was trespassing.

Carl buzzed Rios from the lab. Rios picked up his fresh mug of Brazilian coffee and went in.

"Doctor Griffith, this the Honorable Captain Rios." The two men shook hands. Griffith was young, couldn't be any older than twenty-nine. He was tall, had brown-blond hair with a prep-school cut, deep brown eyes, gold rimmed perfectly round glasses and a walrus mustache. He had on a blue Stanford twill shirt, leather vest, black jeans and black gold-tipped boots.

"How goes the medical profession?" Rios inquired.

"Overworked, over-rated, and over done. Doc Tapia was holding up a tremendous work load. I've requested two interns to come and help out. This town is something. Alcala is too far to send anyone for an emergency and the people out here still expect house calls. I never knew some of the Indians wouldn't go to the hospital. Doc Tapia was a miracle worker in my book."

Rios sat on the lab stool. "Do you think you would like to stay here?"

Carl interrupted. "Captain, take a look at this?" He held up the magnifying glass to Rios. "Remember the photo of Hava? He was a slight man, maybe five feet two at the most. Well, the guy in this photo is at least five eight and the body is that of a twenty year old.

Doctor Griffith lit up his pipe, "How much do you want to bet the body is Alex Cruz?" Griffith pointed to the long legs and the dark muscular chest. Rios followed the lines with the magnifying glass.

"Cruz could never get anything on Hava. Alex said Hava never used dope, only alcohol and his wife wouldn't let him drink in the house. Do you think Hava let this get to him and agreed to pay Cruz off?"

Rios handed Carl the magnifying glass. "Hava wasn't killed by either Cruz or

Alex.''

Carl and Griffith stared at each other. The phone rang. Carl picked it up, ''It's for you.'' He handed it to Rios.

''Mr. Brusher, yes. Well, we're still trying to retrieve the money.'' Carl quickly wrote out a message on the paper next to the phone and handed it to Rios.

''Yes. I understand. Carl just handed me a note, yes. The money is in the safe here. It was found in the drug pusher's car. If you want to send a man to pick it up, Carolyn will write you up a receipt.''

Rios hung up, ''It's time I met the new member of the group. Where's Floyd?''

Carl rolled up the photo. ''Why wouldn't Cruz kill Hava?'' Rios was already walking out the door and down the hall.

''Two things don't mesh. One, Hava was all around town with different women for whatever reason. Just the thing for Cruz and his hunger for black knowledge.'' Rios liked that term. Mary Quintana really had a way with words. Rios stopped. The front office was empty. ''Although, I can't believe Hava was ever unfaithful to his wife in the true meaning of the word. Two, is that Hava was not about to swallow a capsule, any capsule that someone handed him. He was a private man. It is too much of an assumption that he took the pill as an effort to sober up for his wife. Besides, I never heard of such a pill. Also, Cruz and Hava did not travel in the same circles. If Cruz was trying to get to Hava, do you think Hava would just pop any capsule Cruz handed to him?''

''Then these other murders were coincidental?''

Rios leaned against Carolyn's desk, ''More or less, although they are related through Cruz.''

''Captain, Floyd and Carolyn went for coffee at the bakery.''

''Carl, let's head out to the Pueblo. There are some things I need to see for myself.''

Doctor Griffith called out to them. He was getting into his cream colored Jeep. ''Jerez certainly is a hot bed of coals, isn't it?''

Rios frowned, ''Well, stay awhile, it might grow on you.'' He waved as the doctor drove off.

Rios and Carl were thoughtful on the drive. The houses around the plaza were deserted with only dogs wandering in the cold wind.

The road was bumpy in spots. The Public Service had come in this summer past and put in septic tanks and the main pipes went directly under the road. The ZIA had not contracted the road crew to come and grade the road smooth. They drove down the hill, over the bridge, over the dirt road and up to the chickens clucking in Cruz's yard.

''You take the photography room, I'll look around.'' Rios pointed to the house.

"Okay," agreed Carl. Rios walked over to the shed, the chickens followed him.

"I'll feed you if there's anything to feed you with." Rios pulled out two large burlap sacks. The one in his right hand was heavy, he almost dropped it. The other dribbled grain over his boots. Rios threw the grain sack out into the yard.

Rios watched, "Wouldn't Moses love to meet you girls."

Rios turned his attention on the other sacks. He opened one, rolling down the sides. It was full of papers, metal frames, and something that felt like rocks. Rios laid it out on the ground, developing paper and metal frames for the photos. Rios put them in the back of the truck.

He pulled out the rest of the sacks. They were either full of grain or almost empty. Carl had gone through the shed before, so the sacks were neater than Rios remembered.

The floor of the shed was covered with grain, chicken droppings, and sawdust. Rios knelt down and examined the sawdust and scooped some into a pouch. He brushed the floor with an empty burlap sack. Dust flew around his head and he stood up sneezing.

"Something tells me what we're looking for is in here somewhere. Cruz is a sneak, he wouldn't leave things lying around the house."

Rios stomped his heel hard on the floor. It was wood. He pushed the dry grain and dirt off the floor. Planks appeared. Rios knelt down, pulled on a loose piece. It moved. Under it was more dirt.

Rios continued to pull and more dirt and grain filled the air. Suddenly he hit a board that was nailed down.

He used another board for leverage and pushed hard. The board groaned, then broke loose, knocking Rios over. He regained his balance and peered into the hole, neatly placed rolls of paper. There was a large folded paper in the bottom.

"What did you find?" Carl asked, sticking his head into the fog of dust.

"I'm not sure. Here, take it into the light."

Rios stood up, his head bent down to avoid the sloping roof, and came out into the sunlight, brushing off his jeans.

"Captain, I think you found it." Carl unrolled the largest paper, a picture of Doc handing Alex Cruz two large bundles and Alex handing Doc thick bundles of bills.

"Where did you find this? We went through all that stuff this morning?"

"Under the floor."

Carl grinned, "We thought the floor was dirt."

Rios took out his handkerchief and wiped his face, "It was wood, I took it all up. What did you find in the house?"

Carl shook his head, "Nothing of value, Cruz's old family album, Alex's school books, some canned food, and a bundle of letters. They're from a woman to Cruz. Here they are." Carl handed the letters to Rios. He shoved them into his pocket.

"Let's examine these when we get back to headquarters. We better hurry if we want to catch the ZIA. They walk out of their office at twelve-thirty and it's almost that now."

The ZIA office was next to the plaza in the Pueblo. Rios parked the truck next to the church and the two men walked across the road. The door was new white pine with fancy gold handles.

Rios pushed it open and stepped down into a modern expensive interior. The rug on the floor was Navajo woven in bright red and white triangles.

The furniture was stretched white plastic. The whiteness gave the appearance of tissue paper. The coffee table was glass with wrought iron legs. The lamp over their heads was a large bulb with hundreds of mirrors. A secretary sat behind a desk in one corner.

Paper work was everywhere. The young woman had long black hair, an expensive soft green dress, and bright red finger nails. She had her back to them, holding the ear piece of the phone in long slender fingers.

"Well, I told him if he would go to Alcala without me, he could just stay there. What did you think I would say?"

Rios cleared his throat, his hat dripped grain every time he turned his head. Carl put his hand on Rios' shoulder and pointed to the fireplace in the corner. On the hearth was a kachina. Next to it was a framed photo. It was the same photo of Hava that stood on the bureau in Hava's bedroom.

Ray Hava was written on the bottom in red. Carl turned the kachina on its side. The arm fell off but Rios grabbed it before it hit the floor.

"Well, Susan, I think it's terrible they way he throws his body around." The secretary kept talking. Rios glanced at her. She was still turned away from them.

Rios' eyes widened as Carl pulled a bank roll of money from the hollow arm of the kachina. The two men smiled.

There was over a thousand dollars. Rios handed it back to Carl, motioning him to put the money back.

"Well, I don't think it's fair. Give me a man with a lot of money and warm bedside manner and I'll follow him anywhere." Rios smiled. Carl put the kachina back on the hearth.

Rios walked over to the secretary's desk, "Excuse me, Miss, could we have word with you?"

She turned abruptly, "Yes, sir, I'll get right on the case. Talk to you around five. Yes, sir, good-bye." She hung up and swung around in her white chair, "How may I help you?"

Carl held his smile until they were in the truck. "Rios, you have real style.

How did you do that? I still can't believe you."

Rios chuckled, "She fell for it, didn't she. Well, she deserved it. You hold that kachina. We don't want that arm to fall off. It was a superstition I read about in a book. Maybe it's true. So be careful."

Carl took the kachina out of his jacket. "She fell for it all right. How did you know they took this the day of Hava's death?"

Rios looked in the rear view mirror, the ZIA Police were pulling up in their fancy car.

"Just a minute, let me talk to Old Grandpa. He's sitting in the Plaza. We have to get away with this. We're still on the reservation and the ZIA has arrived."

Carl swallowed, "Ah-oh."

Old Grandpa was sitting on the thick edge of the old cement watering hole in the middle of the plaza. His grey felt hat leaned forward over his brow. A deep brown cane swung from his wrist. He turned as Rios approached.

"Hello, how's life treating you?"

"The green policeman. What are doing here?"

"Trying to stay out of trouble. What are you doing here, Old Grandpa?"

"Watching the ZIA. They allow the sewers to be in the Pueblo, right under the hard ground of our people." Old Grandpa pointed to his feet. "I never thought that stuff would run through our sacred dancing ground." He shook his head.

Rios shielded his eyes from the sun. He could make out the figure of Martinez and Tapia from the ZIA moving towards them.

"Does it hurt the Pueblo to have the sewer go through?" Old Grandpa stood up, his chest swelled, "Yes, I am of the old people, we took great care to keep our Pueblo clean." He hit the ground with his cane.

Rios heard the ZIA men coming closer. He asked Old Grandpa, "Does the ZIA know how you feel about this?"

Old Grandpa didn't hear him, "Get, you green policeman, get down on your knees and smell over here." He tapped the ground with his cane.

Rios hesitated. Old Grandpa was not someone the ZIA would like to tangle with, Rios got down on all fours.

He tipped his head forward, grains of chicken food fell forward onto Old Grandpa's boot. "Over here, do you smell that? That is not what our Great Up Above Spirits want under our feet when we dance to their honor. Now, follow it over here, isn't that a stink?" Old Grandpa started chuckling. "You trying to catch eagles with that grain? It won't work, they don't like green policemen."

Rios followed the cane on his hands and knees. The ZIA men approached, started laughing at Rios but he did not respond.

"You, you two, who are so hot in your fancy cars and your fancy outfits. You two, with the big smiles on your faces. You should be the ones to smell what you have done to our Pueblo." Old Grandpa shouted at them. People going in and out of the Mercantile came to see what was going on. The women who were sitting inside their mud stacked homes came out to hear Old Grandpa's complaint.

"You get down and smell what you have done to our Pueblo. To the sacred dancing grounds. If the policeman from the town can smell, you better get down and smell your Pueblo." He stabbed at the ground. The ZIA men edged forward.

Old Grandpa glared at them as they knelt. "Smell over here." Old Grandpa led them across the square. Rios slowly stood up. The ZIA men were too busy to notice him now.

Rios eased over to the truck. "What's going on over there?" Carl asked, clutching the kachina.

"Old Grandpa is what is going on over there. He always has a good joke up his sleeve. This time it's a legitimate complaint. He doesn't like the sewers going through the dancing grounds. He has the ZIA men smelling the sewer line."

"Did you smell it?"

"No, can't smell a thing. Although the ZIA men will probably smell something before the afternoon is over."

* * * * *

Rios and Carl joked as they went up the stairs. Carolyn's chair was empty.

"Bet she's having fun." Carl pointed to the chair.

"Well, let's hope it isn't as risky as what we did. I bet Old Grandpa has the ZIA men still out there smelling the ground." They took the kachina into the lab.

* * * * *

Carolyn put her right hand on Floyd's arm her left hand pointed a finger to the cedar post fence. They stayed low and listened.

"There's nothing wrong, should there be?" Her dark reddish brown hair blew out behind her, eyes glowing in the sunlight.

"You're upset. But then we know how you behave, you have a short temper, ever since you were little, lied for your own benefit, resentful of the rest of us, so let's not play games."

She turned her head. Carolyn covered her face. Did the young girl see them?

"If you know so much about me, why do you bother to have anything to do with me? If I have always been the same and you refuse to let me change, then you write the lines and I'll say them."

"You've always been full of anger at us. I don't know why. You have all this hostility. When will it ever stop?"

"Stop? Do you want it to stop? You seem to be content in your misery. If things are not in a turmoil you push, prod, shove, manipulate and upset so that you can sit back and glow in the warmth and the hostility of others." The young woman put her hands on her slender hips, her white cotton dress flared out at the waist. The wide gold belt complimented a striking figure.

"You love to hurt and be hateful to us. Well, go back to Evelyn Hava and let her teach you photography. You will have a hard life, daughter of mine, you make life difficult for all of those that come in contact with you. You go back and let her be your mother and let her teach you. Now that her poor dear husband is dead, you can go live with her."

The young girl lifted her hand, "How can you say such things. He lied, he hurt her, he cheated on her, he kept money from her. She hurt, hurt something awful, he is better dead. Goodbye. Don't bother to say you're sorry." She swung her hand down, silver bracelets jangling.

The young girl grabbed her purse and ran down the path the to her small red MG. She revved the engine and sailed out of sight as Floyd and Carolyn pushed open the wooden gate.

Mrs. Tapia was opening the door when Carolyn called to her.

"We're sorry to bother you, but we'd like to ask a few questions." Floyd pulled out his Police I.D. and handed it to Mrs. Tapia.

Carolyn watched the woman's face. It was hardened by the conversation with her daughter. She attempted a smile, failed, then pushed the front door open.

"Please come in. Doc's not in, if that's who you would like to speak to."

Carolyn touched Mrs. Tapia's shoulder gently. "It is you we need to talk with. Do you know why Nee-nee was asked to stay with you?"

Her eyes welled up with tears, "How is she? We miss her bright face. No, I don't know. Why?"

"She's fine. Her father came. Do you know how he was notified?"

Mrs. Tapia went up the step from the front room into the living room. Kachinas stood in a row on the fireplace hearth. They all appeared to be Hava's.

"My husband knew her father. His wife was deathly ill. This was when we lived north of Baltimore years ago. My husband was an intern at the time, a specialist in woman's diseases. He helped her; Nee-nee's mother, that is. Poor woman died several years later." Mrs. Tapia bowed her head. "Mothers do die, don't they?"

"Yes, they do. Mine did. Mothers are very important, alive."

"I suppose. Nee-nee came out here and her father kept an eye on her through my husband. Has she gone with him?"

"No. At present he's in the jail in Alcala."

Floyd broke in. "Well, we best go. Thank you for your time." Carolyn shook her hand and pushed her co-worker out in front of her.

Dan had moved to the hall to listen in on the conversation. His sister was crazy to hurt his mother. Now everyone was in for a good surprise with the police being here. His sister had been too harsh. Maybe Uncle Tito was right, his sister *was* a different breed.

Dan slipped through the hall to the front room.

"She said she couldn't love, no she couldn't like herself if she didn't like her parents. Yet, she turns around after condemning us and says she is proud of herself, she likes herself. I can't believe the hate she breathes . . ."

His mother was talking to herself again. She didn't know Doc had been called in for questioning this morning. When she finds that out, his sister will be grand slam trivia.

Dan started the truck and drove away. His mother would not even notice his absence. Who cares about the nice guy, it's the trouble makers that get all the attention.

Suddenly a dust devil hit the side of the truck filling it up with dirt. Dan rolled up the window as the rain started.

San Jaime was a resort, a place of refuge, a silent world of peace to Dan. He drove up Uncle Tito's driveway. Nee-nee was putting flowers on the mama dog's grave. How strong and beautiful she was.

"Dan, what a surprise." Nee-nee didn't smile. Dan's dark face did not need a smile. He sat down on a stump near her and told about the unrest at home. His resentment was with his mother. It began to rain again.

"I love your mother. She is so understanding. Dan, let's get in out of the rain. Did you bring it with you? Or did it know to follow the rain in your heart?"

They went into the kitchen. She turned and held his hand, "Dan, you're un- just in putting the blame on your mom. She's trying to please everyone and get them to cooperate."

"She should try to please herself more and we would make it the best we could. Her advice is always for us. Her thoughts are on us, sometimes I feel I can't breathe around her."

They sat drinking hot mint tea and eating cookies. Dan dropped a chunk of cookie on the floor and reached down to pick it up. "Look at all those ants." Dan lifted his foot to stomp them out.

"No, watch them. See that battered looking one. He's working fast carrying pieces back and forth the wall edge. This one is wandering around with nothing. He keeps bumping into the others."

"They remind me of people. Don't you see that one going only so far then scurrying back? She reminds me of my sister."

Nee-nee frowned, "Let's figure out which one reminds us of someone, but not family. Ants are always boys, only the big fat mama is female."

"Yeah, like big Red." They both laughed.

"Nee-nee, you understand so much about life. I wish I could live with an uncle in a Pueblo in peaceful times."

Nee-nee laughed, "You just told me the other day that since you met me your life has *not* been dull. You contradict yourself, Dan Tapia."

Nee-nee's face blushed. Dan took her hand and held it close to his shirt. "There is a special someone I would like to hold close to me. Do you know anyone who would oblige?"

Nee-nee stared at her lap then closed her eyes. The empty feeling was full; she wanted to run and hide; she wanted to hug him until they became one. Her feelings reeled inside her until she began to feel dizzy.

Dan stood up and pulled her to him. He put his arm around her side and drew her close. She could smell the rain on his shirt. Her head leaned on his shoulder; he kissed her hair.

"The pups are out in the rain." Uncle Tito limped in dragging a burlap sack into the kitchen. He studied the mud floor.

"I'll bring them in." Nee-nee disappeared out the kitchen door. Dan sat down, picking up his mint tea.

"Sell any baskets today?" Dan's cheeks burned.

"Yeah, some." Uncle Tito started to mumble. He opened the door for Nee-nee. The pups were squeaking and shaking in their willow basket.

"Here, put them by the fire." Dan took them and placed them in the rounded corner by the wood stove.

"Nee-nee, fix lunch. Dan, you stay. We have to talk about things." Uncle Tito mumbled under his breath and put his hat on the chair. His bald head was red from sunburn, his long braids pulled out of the blue jean waist band. He threw them behind his back.

"Dan, Gerald tells me your sister is staying with Mrs. Hava. Is she?"

Dan let out his breath. He was expecting something all together different. He glanced at Nee-nee. She had a soft smile on her face.

"No. She's not staying with Mrs. Hava. She's living in a house north of the Pueblo. A sick man Dad took care of is now in the Alcala Hospital. So she's staying there to help out."

"Mrs. Hava is meeting with her?"

"Oh, yes, they've been good friends for a long time. Mrs. Hava is teaching my sister photography. Everyone knows that. She also gets the medication Mrs. Hava needs although my dad doesn't know about it."

Uncle Tito rubbed his chin, shook his head, then looked at the clock.

Nee-nee served hot posole and tortillas. They ate in silence.

Uncle Tito put his plate up by the bucket in the sink. "You best get to school, half a day gone." He shuffled over to his basket and started working. Dan and Nee-nee cleaned up and left in Dan's truck.

*****

Rios met them at the top of the stairs, "Carolyn, did you get a report from the Alcala office yesterday?"

Carolyn took her purse off her arm and walked around her desk. "Here you go, it came just as I was leaving."

Rios read it in front of her.

"Carolyn, there are some letters on my desk that belong to Cruz. Each of them is the same. In each letter there is a photo of the same woman in the same pose. Look at them and tell me what you think?"

Carolyn walked around Floyd following Rios to his desk in the office. Rios gathered up the bundle of light blue envelopes and dumped them in Carolyn's arms.

"Is that Floyd out there?"

Carolyn blushed, "Oh, I'm sorry, I should have introduced you."

Rios smiled, "That's all right. I figured it out for myself. How did it go at the Tapia's?"

"Mrs. Tapia was having a fight with her older daughter. I guess her daughter is taking photography lessons from Mrs. Hava. Also, Doc was an old friend of Nee-nee's parents. He treated Nee-nee's mom for some kind of female disorder years ago. Doc contacted Sam to come and help his kid." Carolyn sighed, "Nee-nee's mom is dead."

Rios watched Carolyn walk down the hall. Carolyn's mom had died two years ago and Carolyn still held the pain inside.

"Captain Rios, I'm Floyd Custer. Arrived last night. Glad to be in your squad, Captain." Floyd hesitated. He put his hand up to an almost salute, then saw Rios put his hand out to shake. Floyd gripped Rios' hand with strength. Rios patted Floyd on the back.

"Out here you'll find a gentle handshake will take you further than one with muscle. How's Carolyn treating you?"

Floyd glanced down the hall. "All right. She's very headstrong, but a nice lady. This is some place. The town is spread all over. I guess I better get myself some wheels. I thought you might have a police vehicle."

Rios shook is head. "No, no such luck, buddy." They walked into the lab, Rios still holding the report in his hand. "Carl, it's just as we expected. Cruz was questioned with his lawyer and he denied killing anyone. He admitted to harassment, blackmail and dope pushing. but not killing. They hooked him up to the lie detector and it showed he was telling the truth about not killing. Any ideas?"

Carl looked up from the microscope, "There is one thing bothering me, Cap, where did Cruz get the gelatin capsules? If he used them he would have a large quantity around. He wouldn't just have two or three. Also, the report from the medical examiner in Alcala showed traces of the drug mixed with alcohol in the stomach. The burns in the throat were after death had occurred."

Floyd shook his head again, "Why would his son tell everyone his father showed him how to do it, if his father *didn't* do it?"

Rios put his hand on Floyd's shoulder, "There's no love there. Alex was out for spilled blood ever since his mother left. He had no affection for his father at all."

Floyd's shiny black leather jacket was pulled down by his heavy hands in his pockets. His tan slacks matched his jogging shoes. He was an athlete in a windy, tired town with a murderer on the loose.

"Captain, it isn't like this all year, is it?"

Rios tilted his head at Floyd and smiled. "No, Floyd, actually it's beautiful all summer. The fruit trees bloom in the spring. Birds migrate through here. The summers are glorious in color. But the fall is rough, cold wind fights with the hot air. Summer doesn't like to leave our humble climate. You're not homesick already, are you?"

Rios walked across the hall to his office. Floyd turned around. "Carl, I left a pretty lady behind, that's all. She wants to be a professional designer. I just wanted a pretty lady."

Carolyn knocked lightly on the office door. "Rios, I have a hunch, would you mind if I stepped out for awhile? It should just take an hour so so? I ran a check on the name on the letters with Uncle Tito."

Rios shuffled the papers on the desk, "Where are you going? Want Floyd to go with you?"

Carolyn smiled, "I'm going out and, no, I would like to go alone."

Rios put his hand up to stop her. "Is there anything I should know, before I get a phone call from someone?"

Carolyn chuckled, "No, all the difficult calls have been taken care of. If the Post Office calls, tell them the blue form has been mailed."

"That's all. Fine, just be careful."

Carolyn hurried down the stairs and into the fresh air. She pulled her sleek Ford out into the traffic and drove to the school parking in the lot next to the playground. The school bell rang calling the kids back to classes. She watched in her rearview mirror as they came running out of the big doors of the cafeteria to the main building. A big half-ton truck pulled up as the sun pushed through the clouds.

Nee-nee and Dan got out of the same side of the truck. Carolyn got out of her car and moved through the fast moving crowd to Nee-nee.

"Hello, how are you feeling?" Carolyn touched her shoulder. Nee-nee turned.

"Hi, how are you? Thanks so much for the other day."

"Nee-nee, I need to ask you some questions, if I could?"

"Sure, let's go over to the art room, it's quiet over there. Is it all right if Dan comes along?"

Carolyn nodded and they led the way.

Carolyn sat on one of the low tables. "Here's a photo of a woman, do you know her?" Carolyn handed the photo to Nee-nee as Debbie pushed through the door.

"Well, well, well, if it's not the stranger from the other side of the moon. Where've you been all morning? You're in hot water with the English teacher. Both of you guys."

Debbie looked over Nee-nee's shoulder at the photo. "You know Nee-nee, that woman looks like you. The same eyes. Who is she?"

Nee-nee was fascinated. Was it someone she should know? She felt her head pull trying to think. What a sad expression on her face.

"Hey, you guys, what are you doing in here?" Gerald came through the side door carrying frame and oils. Debbie whispered something under her breath.

"Oh, yeah, let me see, I'm older than any of you guys." Gerald stood behind Nee-nee.

"I've seen her before."

Carolyn turned to him, "Who are you?"

"I'm Gerald Oyea, Ray Hava's stepson. When I was helping my dad, my step-dad, out at the store one time, Alex came in and bought some stuff. He wrote a check. My stepdad gave him a hard time and asked me to get his I.D. on the check. So I asked to see his driver's license. A photo of the same woman was in his wallet opposite the license. Only the woman in the photo he had was holding a little baby with a pink blanket, a pink bow was in her hair with a pink feather in it. I thought it was funny."

Debbie pulled Gerald aside, "Miss, this is my boyfriend and sometimes he's a little weird."

Carolyn lifted the photo from Nee-nee's fingers. "Let me leave a copy with you. It may be nothing. It was just a thought." Carolyn pulled out a xerox copy of the photo and gave it to Nee-nee.

"You better get to class. I don't want to get you in trouble." Carolyn followed them out of the building. Nee-nee was quiet. She couldn't get the face out of her mind.

"Carolyn, let me get permission to go with you to Uncle Tito. He would know who this is. He could help us. I can't concentrate on school work now anyway."

Dan was already on his way to class. Debbie and Gerald had gone to another building.

"All right, I'll go with you."

They met the principal in the hall. His dark eyes sparkled, "More police, am I right?"

Carolyn smiled, "Yes, I need to borrow this girl. Would it be all right?"

The principal put his hand on Nee-nee's shoulder. "On one condition, tomorrow you show up on time and in class."

"I will. If I don't Uncle Tito will give me to the Wind Spirit."

The principal nodded in approval. "Be good." Nee-nee zipped up her blue jacket as they got into the Ford and drove to the Pueblo.

"Does your mom live close by?"

Carolyn checked her side view mirror, "No, my mom lived in Boston. She died two years ago."

Nee-nee put her hand out flat on the seat. "I'm sorry. It must be awful to lose your mother."

"The worst part is, I didn't realize how much she meant to me until she was gone. You expect so much from your parents that at times you never see who they are or what they need."

"I suppose, I never had that problem."

"Certainly you have an image of what they would be like if they came back for you, swimming an ocean or riding through blizzards and the like?"

"Funny, I did think of that."

"Don't tell me, your father disappointed you?"

"Well, as a good friend put it, he didn't disappoint me, my image of him did. Carolyn, could we stop at the Mercantile? It's on the way."

Carolyn smiled. "Sure, do you have some money or do you need to borrow some?"

"No, I have enough." She shoved her long fingers into her sweater jacket's sagging pocket.

Carolyn pulled into the drive by the alley. The front of the Mercantile was swamped with cars and delivery trucks. Nee-nee pulled out four quarters.

"I'll be right back."

"Certainly couldn't be expensive."

Nee-nee ran up the steps into the Mercantile as Carolyn freshened her lipstick, brushed back fluffy red bangs. A car's motor revved behind her and she saw the Tapia girl's red MG zoom around her, honk at a dog and screech to a halt in front of a weathered blue screen door.

"Hi, I'm back with my bargain." Nee-nee slid into the passenger's seat and slammed the door.

"What is that?"

"It's a super large dropper."

"Whatever for?"

"I'm going to use it to feed the pups."

Carolyn shifted the car into reverse and turned her head for one last look at the red MG. "Pups' mother gone dry?"

"It's the Tapia girl at Mrs. Hava's house. She has some nerve. You aren't supposed to park on the plaza unless it's an emergency. What is she doing?"

Carolyn made a mental note. "Did the pups' mother go dry?"

"Their mother died."

Carolyn was lost in thought as they drove the low road out to the north side of the Pueblo. There were driveways after driveways that went to different houses. Some were elaborate with well kept flowers. Others were traditional mud adobe houses with tractors, and red wagons and bikes in the front. As they rode the houses dwindled in substance as did the road.

"Here it is. Back up a little." Nee-nee pointed at a house with a sloping mud roof.

Carolyn pulled in the bumpy drive. Uncle Tito's truck had the hood up.

"Don't worry. It's a good sign. It means Uncle Tito sold enough baskets to get a new starter for the truck."

Carolyn frowned. It must be nice to know where every dollar that comes in will go. Not like trying to decide which pair of party shoes to buy, especially if you never went to parties.

"Let me go and check on the pups. Uncle Tito must be inside. Come on in."

Carolyn followed Nee-nee into the dark mud home. Carolyn noticed the heavy wood door was solid, certainly nothing one would find at the department store. The mud floor was deep red. She had remembered reading how they treated adobe floors with goat's blood to seal the dirt from chipping or scuffing off. Carolyn hesitated as she put her foot down.

"Carolyn, he's in the kitchen. Come and see the pups."

Carolyn noticed a dark room to the left. It had a crude bed in it and some girl's clothing hanging on a wooden peg board that was out of place in the mud environment. She pushed aside a blanket that hung down. On the right was an alcove. It had a bedroll laid out on it and some moccasins. On the wall was another peg board with ceremonial kilts, leggings with bells, and different blankets hanging from it. One blanket was pulled back to a hook on the wall.

Uncle Tito was standing in front of a high banco that had a mud sink in it. In the sink was a bucket of water. Next to that sat an incredible stove, white porcelain with bread warmers coming out over the top of the burners.

Uncle Tito walked over to where Nee-nee was dropping condensed milk down the hungry mouths.

"How is school?"

"Carolyn needs to ask you something. She wanted me to come along."

"I'm Carolyn, we met at the school infirmary. I have a photo here." Carolyn pulled the photo out of her shoulder bag and handed it to Uncle Tito. He reached out to take it, then stopped.

The mechanical device in his hand was covered with a thick slimy substance.

He was rubbing it clean with an old shirt.

"How about if I hold it and you look?" Carolyn suggested.

Uncle Tito nodded. He stopped, stared at the photo, then glanced at Nee-nee. She had stopped her work to watch his expression. He shrugged and walked out to the truck.

Nee-nee stood up. "He knows. He knows who it is."

"I'll go out and see if I can get him to give me a hint. Looks like you've got your work cut out for you, little Mamacita."

Uncle Tito was standing on the front bumper of the truck. His braids were tucked into his suspenders, straw hat tipped back on his head, sleeves rolled up above his elbows.

Carolyn walked to the driver's door and leaned against it. The truck moved, groaned, resigned itself to the added weight. Uncle Tito did not look up as he mumbled, "You know who she is don't you?"

Carolyn didn't respond. Uncle Tito pulled a wire loose and stretched to shove a piece of machinery in the hole.

"She's a relation of Cruz." Uncle Tito whispered.

Carolyn lifted her shoulder bag higher on her shoulder.

"The woman is Cruz's wife." Carolyn's eyebrows knitted as she held her breath steady.

"Cruz's wife left him for another man, in the east."

Carolyn shifted her weight.

"Cruz's wife married Nee-nee's father." Carolyn watched Uncle Tito reach for a wire. He put the wire from his left hand to the wire in his right hand. Suddenly, Uncle Tito jerked, then flew off the truck to the ground with a hard thud.

Nee-nee ran outside.

"Dumb, dumb, dumb."

Nee-nee lifted Uncle Tito's head up. He groaned. His hand was black.

Carolyn lifted Uncle Tito to a sitting position. "Let's get him in my car. We better get him to the Doc."

Nee-nee shook her head, "If he's going to die, let him die here."

"He's not going to die. He got an electrical shock. I shouldn't have bothered him when he was working."

Nee-nee held open the door as Carolyn pulled him into the back seat.

"Jump in. You really should wear warmer clothes. We don't have time to get your jacket. Come on, move."

Carolyn backed the car out and screeched around the corner barely missing an old Buick station wagon.

They went over the big bump and onto the main road that leads through the Pueblo.

"Look, there's Doc's fancy car in front of the Mercantile. I'll run in and get him, Hold on to Uncle Tito."

Carolyn pulled up next to Doc's car and ran into the store.

Strange finding Doc here, so close by. She ran through the store. Charles was cutting meat.

"Charles, where is Doc?" Carolyn walked around the counter. Charles glared at her.

"Not now, Charles I'm not here to buy Sunday's dinner. I have an emergency, I need Doc. Where is he?"

No sooner had the words left her mouth than Doc came out of the back with Mary Quintana.

"Doc, we have an emergency outside. Could you come and help?"

Doc straightened his vest. "Well, that depends on what it is. If this is a police matter, no I can not."

"Come on Doc, this is medical."

He shrugged his shoulders at Mary Quintana and followed Carolyn.

Doc picked up Uncle Tito's wrist, pulled out his vest watch and quietly counted to himself.

"What happened?"

Nee-nee explained, tears rolled down her face. Carolyn leaned against the driver's door tapping her foot.

"What can we do?" Carolyn leaned over.

"Here are my car keys. Get my black bag out of the passenger's side."

"He's all right. The electrical shock stunned him. He's an old coot, it will take more than electricity to knock him into the next world."

Carolyn handed him the black bag and Doc took out a small clear bottle and a syringe.

Carolyn winced. "What is that?"

Doc frowned, "If you are going to ask for my help then you will have to trust me. Let's go in and get something for the burn."

He closed the door on Nee-nee and Uncle Tito. Nee-nee rocked him in her arms as Doc and Carolyn went up the steps to the Mercantile.

"Two bottles of Sunburn Aide." Doc threw four dollars down on the counter. "And a roll of butterscotch lifesavers."

Doc took the bag and turned to Carolyn. "Don't think I'm here for any other reason than medical." Doc was standing right in front of the entrance's wooden screen door.

"Mary's a sick woman. Easily treatable, though. All these years she has suffered from terrible cramps, the once-a-month kind. She was on all kinds of medications."

Carolyn noticed Doc's concern. He was wrinkling up the top of the brown bag that held the medicine.

"I told her to drink tea with ginger and you know what? It worked. Would have saved that woman a lot of trauma if she asked me first."

Outside Uncle Tito was mumbling, his eyes still closed. "Here's some burn medicine. Just spray it on his hands and arm. Don't wrap them, let the air do it's work. He'll be all right soon."

Doc handed the package to Nee-nee. Carolyn thanked the Doc and got into the car. Suddenly, a car screeched in her direction, then skidded. Doc puffed out his chest and hurried over to the car.

"What do you think you're doing, young lady?"

The red MG backed up and stopped. "Dad, what a nice surprise meeting you here."

"Mercedes, get out of that car this instant. What in blazes do you think you're doing? This is a Pueblo, not a race track."

She pushed her hair back and jumped out of the car over the door. She wore a white fiesta blouse and tight black slacks.

"Dad, you gave me this car to drive, remember. It's my car. I was not racing, merely rushing."

Carolyn frowned. Nee-nee tapped Carolyn on the shoulder. "Can we go home now?"

Carolyn drove slowly down the dirt road, over the bump, and into the driveway. The old truck stood in its same sorrowful position.

The two women got Uncle Tito situated on his bedroll.

"Carolyn, thank you for helping us."

"Never crossed my mind not to."

"She's my mother, right?"

"Yes, I guess it looks that way."

"Anybody else's?"

"Why would she be anyone else's?"

"Why would Alex Cruz have a picture of the woman in his wallet?"

"Because he is her son."

"I can't believe my mother is Alex's mom."

"She was married to Cruz. Couldn't stay with him, so she left for the big city and your father."

"Some woman, poor taste in men."

Nee-nee held the photo up to the light from the small kitchen window.

"Do you think she's pretty?"

Nee-nee put the photo down. She poured hot water over mint and handed Carolyn a mug.

"Well, just between us, I think she is very pretty. Not stunning like you, but close. You have her coloring, although your eyes are deep set like Uncle Tito's."

"Uncle Tito's?"

"Yes, he really is your uncle. Your mom's mother was Uncle Tito's sister."

"The one that died in the plane crash?"

"None other."

The two drank tea in silence. The old clock on the shelf ticked away as Nee-nee stared at the photo. Carolyn worried about Uncle Tito and the medicine Doc had injected.

Suddenly the front door resounded with a heavy knock. Nee-nee turned awkwardly, staring at Carolyn.

"I'll get it, you check on Uncle Tito." Carolyn walked to the door. It pushed open at her touch. "Rios, what a nice surprise."

Rios hurried into the kitchen. "Where is he?" Nee-nee came out from behind the blanket that separated Uncle Tito's bedroll from the kitchen.

"He's in here." She pointed to the blanket. Rios stopped.

"Is he all right." Nee-nee nodded. The alarm on Rios' face stopped her from saying more.

"What is it, Rios?" Carolyn picked up a loose pup and put it in the basket with the others.

"Mercedes Tapia, Doc's daughter, was supplying drugs to Mrs. Hava. Doc called us from the Pueblo this afternoon. He was in a rage. Mary Quintana called us soon after. Doc had a stroke outside the Mercantile. His daughter just drove off and left him there."

Nee-nee and Carolyn both sat down on the same chair as Rios walked over to the crackling stove.

"Doc's in critical at the hospital. When he gets better they will move him to Alcala. Mary Quintana told me about you being there and Doc treating Uncle Tito. I came right away."

Nee-nee stared into Carolyn's eyes.

"Do you know what Doc gave Uncle Tito?" They both shook their heads. "He is breathing?"

Nee-nee lifted up her chin, "Yes, maybe we can awaken him."

She lifted the blanket. Uncle Tito was rocking from side to side.

"Nee-nee, get the medicine Doc gave you. Maybe his arm hurts."

"Uncle Tito, it's Rios. You all right? Can you talk to us? Open your eyes." Rios put his arm under Uncle Tito's head.

Uncle Tito opened his eyes and moaned. Carolyn lifted up his arm and sprayed the medicine on it.

Nee-nee spoke to him in the Indian language. Uncle Tito answered.

"He wants to be left alone. The spray helped the pain. He said he feels all right, only tired."

The three went out and left him alone.

"Nee-nee, why are so many people in the Pueblo into photography?"

"Well, there are only two I know of. One was Cruz, he was into some really wild stuff, and Mrs. Hava. She was a photography major in college. She did all the photos for Ray Hava's resumes and catalogs."

"Did you know about the naked photos?"

Nee-nee rubbed her hands together, "Yes, Uncle Tito showed me some of Cruz's art work. He warned me to stay away from him. The only thing we could figure out was that it was some kind of blackmail idea. The only drawback was that the painter woman from San Thomas wanted to be blackmailed."

Nee-nee pulled herself up on the table and swung her legs over the side. "Well, this is not anything for sure, but the woman wants out of San Thomas. Her husband is a big politician. He's big, tall, and fat and from what I understand a pushy politico. She's fed up with it. He drives around in a poor man's broken down VW and he insists they live in a traditional home in the Pueblo. Her art work is famous but she wants to reap the rewards of her work, so she would like to leave and live in a nice house in Alcala."

"What does that have to do with blackmail?"

"Well, Gerald, that's Debbie's boyfriend, Hava's stepson, thought if she showed that photo of Cruz's to her husband he would divorce her or leave his post. But he didn't do either. He hasn't done anything, unless he gave money to Cruz."

Rios smiled, "If he did that, her plan backfired in her face. Conniving women, they keep popping up. Nee-nee, what do you think of Mrs. Hava?"

Carolyn cleared her throat. She interrupted, "Nee-nee, if you are tired, tell us and we will leave you two alone?"

Nee-nee glanced towards the blanket. "No, I like the company."

Carolyn jumped down from the banco and restoked the wood stove. She filled the pan with water and put it on to boil. Nee-nee explained that Uncle Tito and Mrs. Hava were once good friends. They would joke around and have good talks about old times. Then Cruz started moving into the Pueblo. He wasn't supposed to be on Indian land. But he came into the Mercantile to buy cigarettes and then he would flirt with the girls and one thing led to another. He moved in.

"Well, the more Cruz was around, the less Uncle Tito would talk about seeing Mrs. Hava. Ray and Uncle Tito were on the best of terms. One wouldn't know it the way they stabbed at each other with dirty remarks, but they were like kids."

Carolyn poured tea into the mugs and served them around. She opened the old brown ice box and pulled out some tortillas and laid them flat on the bare stove to heat.

"Well, Mrs. Hava became indifferent to everyone. The ZIA were nice to her for some reason. But Uncle Tito said it was because she wanted a good alibi for evil magic."

Carolyn handed each a hot tortilla. "Evil magic, does that still exist out here?"

Rios gave Carolyn a cold stare. "Oh, yes, now that you mention it, I remember well a cold night down by the river."

"The Clan is not bad. But there is a different organization of women in the Pueblo. They are the social organizers. If someone does something they don't like, they let them know it in a not very nice way."

"Mrs. Hava was in the group of women who did this?"

"Uncle Tito would know more than I would. Mrs. Hava was big into medicines. She would give herbs and teas to the sick for cures. She is highly thought of in the Pueblo for her cures in the old way. Some really fear crossing her for her magic is strong."

Carolyn looked behind the blanket. "Rios, Uncle Tito is awake. I think he wants to talk to you."

Uncle Tito's eyes sparkled again. He waved Rios to kneel down.

"Nee-nee knows about her father. Can Nee-nee stay with me until you decide where she should go?" Uncle Tito's voice was tense.

"Uncle Tito, she knows you are her real uncle. You are her next of kin. She will remain with you as long as you want."

Uncle Tito sighed as Rios moved back into the kitchen. The two were putting out a scrabble game. Carolyn glanced at him.

"Is he all right?"

"Yes, I think I'll go back to the office and check in. Do you want to stay here for a while?"

Carolyn pulled out her key chain.

"Here is the key to my house. If you would just stop by on your way home and turn on the living room light I think I'll stay. I love to play scrabble and the competition is asking for it."

Rios picked up his hat and left them to their game.

*****

The light shone under the lab room door. Rios pushed the door open to find Carl sitting on the lab stool watching the sunset.

Purple clouds were drifting forward turning a soft shade of pink, then yellow, and at last dull white. The wind had stopped, the rain had moved on, and the night was going to be still. Still and quiet, for the sky was hurrying with its load of loud thunder and drenching rains to another land.

"Carl, any news?"

"No. Sam is wanted in three other states."

"Any new evidence?"

"No, it's got to be the Hava woman."

"Why?"

"She was giving Hava vitamin E pills, they're gelatin capsules. The stuff comes right out. Easy to refill."

"Hard to prove. We have to be sure."

"She's alone. She is really alone."

"Doc's daughter, Mercedes, do you think she knows?"

"No. Evelyn Hava is alone. She must know we would come back to her."

"Where's your pipe?"

"I left if over there on the table."

"You want it?"

"No. I'm all smoked out."

"What's going on with you, Carl?" Carl tapped on the window. His hand swept across his high forehead to wipe back the hair that wasn't there.

"It's hard to imagine the loneliness."

"You live alone."

"I have no choice."

"No choice? You could find yourself a lady and settle down."

"No, I don't have that choice. It takes a lot of effort to live with someone. To thrive on the passages of each other's feelings. To talk when you don't want to, to make love when you don't want to, to eat food not of your liking. I couldn't do it. I'm a loner."

Rios struck a match on the underside of the lab table and lit the cigarette hanging from his lips. He threw his hat on the chair in the corner and pulled up the other lab stool to sit next to Carl. The white clouds turned to grey-black.

"There's a difference between being alone and feeling alone."

"Oh, yes, the loneliness and the aloneness of life."

"No, there's a difference of living with someone and being alone. You can live what you want and still share with someone without the problems you speak of."

"That's it. A facade of untruths."

"What untruths?"

"Do you know when I was a baby and my little brother was newborn, well I wasn't a baby then I guess. I was about four. Do you know what my mom would say?"

"No." Rios let out a sigh.

"When my brother would cry all the time my mom would say she wished she could just throw him out the window. Let someone else put up with his screaming."

"Baby's screaming can do that to people."

"Well, why did she put up with it?"

"Do you remember the case we had last year where the neighbor called and told us about a child abuse? We went over there and found a mother spanking her little boy for all she was worth and the little boy wasn't crying or even in pain?"

"Yeah, you turned and walked out."

"The side you take can be the wrong side too often. I felt that mother who was crying and spanking her boy, and not very hard either, was somehow being punished by her kid. Somehow that kid had a hold over her and drove her to such pain that she spanked the kid. What do you think that mother should have done?"

"Thrown him out the window."

"No, seriously, what do you think she should have done? Should she have walked away? Do you think she could have?"

"What are you getting at?"

"That mother loved her son very much. He knew how to hurt her badly, emotionally, and she was caught. It didn't matter what the boy did, it was how he did it. He really hurt her to the point where all she could do was to strike out."

"So, where does that put right and wrong?"

"Well, everyone has a line of tolerance. That line shouldn't be crossed. If you are pushed past that line, the person who has pushed you there is aware of it and you are in trouble. It gives that person control over you."

"What does that have to do with facade?"

"If you are too eager to please and to get along with the person you are living with, you have put yourself close to that line. You yourself have made yourself vulnerable. Your vulnerability has jeopardized your comfort. Anything the other person does will push you closer to that line. Your facade is in jeopardy. The tenseness is what kills your relationship. Not you or your woman can live up to that facade."

"But you had the mother come in for counseling at the Public Health Department?"

"Yeah, someone had to help her. Her husband was gone and her kid was controlling her life. She was miserable with guilt and now she has someone who can help her decide whether she wants to spank her kid or walk away from him."

"I'm still a loner."

"Fine. At least we both know that. Now how will we get to Mrs. Hava?"

"The only way I know of is the capsules. Let me show you my plan."

Carl walked over to the lab table and pulled out a notebook from the top drawer.

"How did you decide to get along with Marge? You're a loner, too?"

"I didn't. She decided to get along with me. Besides, I found out we don't like the same things."

The phone rang. It was Marge, dinner was cold. Carl frowned, "Well, I guess she doesn't like it warm either. See you tomorrow."

Friday: Day 8

Floyd paced back and forth across the kitchen floor. Rios watched his boots as he placed them one in front of the other. The heels were worn on the outside.

Rios turned. The curtains were billowing into the kitchen. There were no screens on the window. Mrs. Hava said she had to run an errand at the Mercantile. They could wait. She wouldn't be but a moment. That moment was an hour and a half ago.

Floyd studied the kitchen counter. Jars of flour, sugar, honey, seeds, beans, and coffee were stair-stepped on top of each other on the counter by the sink, next to the refrigerator.

Rios lit another cigarette. Floyd stopped pacing and leaned against the doorway to the front room.

"Smoking ain't good for you, Cap."

"No, it isn't. Neither is arresting people. Where do you think she is?"

"She's in the Merc. She went over there and she ain't gonna come out."

Rios raised his eyebrow. He doubted the last statement. Somehow he had a feeling she was waiting for them to start going through her things. That she had the place watched. Any suspicious move and the ZIA would be coming through the door.

Rios watched Floyd lean out the window. Floyd was a nice guy, but he didn't know a thing about people. He would learn.

"Maybe it's a good thing this kachina man is dead."

"Why do you say that?"

"Well, kachinas are a superstition, aren't they? I mean now with the knowledge of God and all, folks don't still believe in kachinas do they?"

Rios looked around the room for an ashtray, only his eyes moving. He wasn't going to move from the place he had perched when Mrs. Hava left.

Rios asked him, "Do you believe in God over everything else?" Floyd pushed his hat back. It was new, too wide and somehow a stetson on Floyd didn't fit his personality. "My brother was saved by the Almighty. He was a real loser and he found God and was saved. I don't think kachinas would have helped him much."

"No, I don't suppose they would. Although I'm not one to cross any belief. If it works for someone that's great."

"There are some great looking dames around here." Floyd pulled the curtain back to watch a young girl walking across the plaza.

"Do you see anyone out there with a brown uniform?" Rios whispered.

"No, there are some brown cars parked over on the other side of our truck, but there are no brown clothesmen."

Rios smiled. He'd never heard that term before. "Do you see Mrs. Hava?"

"No. I bet she split. She knows we're on to her."

"We'll wait it out. Let's give her another hour." Floyd turned around, facing him, "She's coming carrying a large sack of groceries. There are two brown clothesmen following her."

The front door thumped. Both men turned to the kitchen door. It was pushed open by Mrs. Hava.

"Sorry to be so long. There were a lot of people." Floyd reached out to help with the bag of groceries but his eye caught Rios shaking his head.

She pushed the groceries onto the counter between the sink and the refrigerator. She brushed back her bangs and sat down opposite Rios. The two of them stared at each other without speaking.

Floyd cleared his throat. "Mrs. Hava, I'm Floyd . . ."

Rios interrupted him. "Mrs. Hava, would you please tell us one more time what happened on the night your husband was killed."

Her voice was calm as she retold of the morning her husband was found dead. Her manner gentle, her eyes cautious, hands firmly placed on the table in front of her.

Rios held his attention on her. "Mrs. Hava, we would appreciate your best ideas on what happened."

She glared at him. Emotions were beginning to swell. "If you know what happened, why ask me?"

Floyd coughed. She gave him a threatening glance. Her soft eyes now burning. "Why do you keep coming back here? Didn't you get all the evidence you needed?"

A car horn honked twice in succession, almost in reply. Floyd quickly looked out the window and winked at Rios. It was Carl's notice that he was on his way to the ZIA headquarters.

Rios rolled a cigarette up and down his fingers. "You tell us?"

Mrs. Hava stood up, drew a deep breath and walked out of the room. Floyd watched Rios but Rios kept rolling the cigarette up and down his fingers. They could hear Mrs. Hava rustling in the next room. Neither moved to see what she was doing. The air was tight, wired with strain.

Mrs. Hava returned and stood in front of Rios. "Your other man is at the ZIA. He drove up. Don't you want to talk to him?"

"No. He has an appointment with the ZIA. It's about a kachina. A kachina with a lot of money in it."

"A kachina? They don't keep kachinas in the office?" Her tone changed, not so steady.

"Evidently, someone turned in a kachina. I'm sure that he can handle it."

Mrs. Hava turned quickly, her eyes searched the room. She went to the bag of groceries and started to put them away.

"What do you want here?" She spoke over her shoulder. Rios nodded to

Floyd. He walked over to her. "Ma'am, I'm new on the case. It seems your husband was taking some sort of medication. Would it be possible for us to see this medication?"

Mrs. Hava backed away, "He wasn't taking any medication. I would know if he was."

Floyd moved forward. "Well, Ma'am, we know for a fact he was taking some vitamin E and that he had badly burned himself at one point."

She held her breath, then gave Rios a searching glance, "Who is this man? He's not from around here?"

Rios frowned, "No. He's from Texas and he's our new member of the Jerez Police Force. His name is Floyd Custer and I can assure you Mrs. Hava, that the name fits him."

Mrs. Hava pulled her hands apart. "I won't be threatened. You really don't have any jurisdiction here. This is Indian land."

Rios stood up, his legs thankful for the movement. "Mrs. Hava, we were called in by the ZIA to investigate this murder. It's an unusual situation. We are all uncomfortable with it. If you will cooperate, we can get to the bottom of this and be done with it."

Someone knocked on the front door. Mrs. Hava opened it with hope in her eyes. Carl stood there with two of the ZIA men. In his hand was the kachina. Mrs. Hava backed away from the door.

Rios was the one who invited them in. Mrs. Hava sat down in the rocking chair by the fireplace, her face white.

"The vitamin E capsules are in the chest. There." She pointed to the chest opposite the front door.

The ZIA men were quiet. Floyd and Carl went over and lifted off the blanket putting it on the floor and opened the chest.

"Well, Ma'am, you certainly do collect the most interesting things."

Floyd lifted out a photo enlarger, sheets of white photo paper, yellow boxes of powder, small pint sized bottles of fluids, and flat photographs. Floyd lifted them out one at a time.

The ZIA men held their positions as they watched photo after photo come up of different people in different poses, none flattering or decent. Mrs. Hava had some of the same ones Cruz had taken including the photo of Hava's face with Alex's body.

Mrs. Hava sat glaring at the kachina now held by Rios.

"You told me you would keep it for me. That money is mine and there is no way you can take that money from me. I earned it."

She leaped up and grabbed the kachina out of Rios' hand. The arm fell to the ground and she dropped on her knees to retrieve it. She bumped into one of the ZIA officers who was the first to find it. She swung at him and he stood up and backed away, his breathing fast, fear in his eyes.

"You give that back to me. It's mine."

Rios nodded and the ZIA officer handed it to her. She struggled with it but there was no money. She threw the arm to the floor.

"Where is it? Where is my money? I earned that. Everytime he went out on me, every time he flirted with another woman, every time he left me here alone, that was my payment. It's mine. I will kill for it and you know it."

She pointed her finger at the ZIA men as they pushed out the door. She was fuming with hate.

Rios placed the kachina down on the hearth; the empty place now filled.

"It's over. I'm afraid you will have to come with us." Rios watched the hate in her eyes turn to fear as she slumped down on the banco.

Carl pulled out pouches for the chemicals that were too big to carry. They loaded the sacks from Carl's case and carried the evidence to the truck.

"Floyd, you drive my truck back. Mrs. Hava and I will go with Carl. Be careful." Rios handed Floyd the keys.

"Of course, sir, I won't wreck it."

Mrs. Hava took her purse and shawl and followed the men to Carl's Pontiac. People were standing all around. Rios shook his head, there was always an audience in the Pueblo. They drove in silence.

Saturday: Day 9

"You mean to say Mrs. Hava had promised to marry Cruz when the affair was over?"

"Yes, only she took Cruz to the cleaners. She had taken the photo equipment to Cruz's house the day before the murder. According to Cruz, she wanted the stuff out of the house when Hava came back. She had put it away, but then decided to move it all out. The strong smell of the developing solution was still in the room. There was no way to open the window and let the smell out."

"She took the stuff over to Cruz's and killed Hava. Why did she want Cruz in on the picture?"

"Well, Cruz was greedy enough to want more money. Her relationship with him was completely one sided, monetary. She wanted Cruz to feel he could trust her completely, so she let him in on her little scam. She let him collect the money and she did the photo work."

"Why didn't Alex say anything about it?"

"He probably didn't know. He was hardly ever home and when he was, he was too drunk to notice."

"Did Mercedes Tapia know about this?"

"That's an unknown. Some of the photos, like the photo of her father, were gathered from some source. All the dirty doings were found out by Mrs. Hava. She and the ladies would gossip. Cruz was made the culprit because he was from outside and no one could touch him, he had a badge."

"What about the money?"

"Cruz didn't know the money was in the kachina. Mrs. Hava told him to take the kachina to the ZIA because it was her favorite. He had no idea he was carrying the sum total of years worth of blackmail money. Possibly some of that money was Hava's that he gave her to pay off Cruz."

"Some lady, what will happen to her now?"

"It's in the hands of the Alcala Courts and the ZIA. However, I don't think they will stand up for her. She did some taboo social no-no's and they're still afraid of her powers. I don't think they want her back."

Carolyn knocked on the door, "Rios, Jose says that the red-headed crazy-talking garage mechanic stole all the good parts off the towed-in car. Will you talk to him?"

"Sure. Floyd, you better get started on the Indian Pueblo Patrol Guide book. Carl, we better send the photos posthaste to Alcala."

Rios watched the men leave the room, then reached over and grabbed a hot mug of fresh coffee. He leaned back and picked up the phone. "Captain Dominique Rios here."